S0-BMT-077

THE STRANGERS IN THE HOUSE

GEORGES SIMENON (1903–1989) was born in Liège, Belgium. He went to work as a reporter at the age of fifteen and in 1923 moved to Paris, where under various pseudonyms he became a highly successful and prolific author of pulp fiction while leading a dazzling social life. In the early 1930s, Simenon emerged as a writer under his own name, gaining renown for his detective stories featuring Inspector Maigret. He also began to write his psychological novels, or *romans durs*—books in which he displays a sympathetic awareness of the emotional and spiritual pain underlying the routines of daily life. Having written nearly two hundred books under his own name and become the best-selling author in the world, Simenon retired as a novelist in 1973, devoting himself instead to dictating memoirs that filled thousands of pages.

P. D. JAMES is the author of fifteen books of detective fiction. She spent thirty years in various departments of the British Civil Service, including the Police and Criminal Law Department of Great Britain's Home Office. She has served as a magistrate and as a governor of the BBC. In 2000 she celebrated her eightieth birthday and published her autobiography, *Time to Be in Earnest.* The recipient of many prizes and honors, she was created Baroness James of Holland Park in 1991.

THE STRANGERS IN THE HOUSE

GEORGES SIMENON

Translated by
GEOFFREY SAINSBURY

With revisions by
DAVID WATSON & OTHERS

Introduction by
P.D. JAMES

NEW YORK REVIEW BOOKS

New York

THIS IS A NEW YORK REVIEW BOOK
PUBLISHED BY THE NEW YORK REVIEW OF BOOKS
1755 Broadway, New York, NY 10019
www.nyrb.com

First published in France as *Les Inconnus dans la maison*, 1940
First published in Great Britain as *The Strangers in the House*
by Routledge & Kegan Paul Limited, 1951
First published in the United States by Doubleday, 1954

Library of Congress Cataloging-in-Publication Data
Simenon, Georges, 1903–
  [Inconnus dans la maison. English]
  The Strangers in the house / by Georges Simenon ; introduction by
P. D. James.
      p. cm. — (New York Review Books classics)
  ISBN 1-59017-194-2 (alk. paper)
  I. Title. II. Series.
  PQ2637.I531513 2006
  843'.912—dc22

                              2005036189

ISBN-13: 978-1-59017-194-3
ISBN-10: 1-59017-194-2

Printed in the United States of America on acid-free paper.
10 9 8 7 6 5 4 3 2

INTRODUCTION

GEORGES Joseph Christian Simenon is one of the most highly regarded and influential of twentieth-century crime writers and one who more than any other combined a high literary reputation with popular appeal. He was also among the most prolific, with over four hundred novels, seventy-five of which feature his French detective, Maigret. The arithmetic of his achievement is astounding: 193 novels written under his own name and over two hundred under eighteen pseudonyms, with world sales of over 500 million copies in fifty-five languages. He was born in Liège in 1903 to Flemish Catholic parents, and although he was close to his father, he remained estranged from his mother for most of his life. He left school at fifteen and among his first jobs became a crime reporter with the *Gazette de Liège*. His first novel, *Au Pont des Arches*, was published in 1921, the year his father died, and two years later, now married, he had one of his short stories published by Colette for *Le Matin*. He then began writing pulp novels under a variety of pen names. He claimed that it usually took him only two weeks to write his novels in a disciplined discharge of creative energy.

This frantic activity was mirrored by a restless life of change, flight, and exile. Simenon lived much of his childhood under the German occupation of Belgium, and wrote:

When I was 11 years old I was rushed down into the cellar because they were shelling the city, and suddenly we all heard cries and a hundred yards away they were rounding up 200 civilians, chosen at random, and shooting them up against the walls of our houses...We were taught to cheat and defraud and lie...and they told us, the children, to carry letters around the town which had come from the other side of the front line, and which a grown-up would have been shot for carrying.

If true, these were useful lessons for a future crime novelist who was to move so confidently in the secret underground of the human heart.

In 1940 Simenon was in France following the German invasion and perhaps in a sense all places were to him occupied territory, streets where he walked alone with the concentrated wariness of a stranger, all his senses alert. His autobiographical works are copious but doubtfully reliable since he tended to alter the facts as he thought expedient, so that a life apparently carefully documented remains in some respects mysterious. It was also a life of contrasts. He was a devoted father and was capable of love, yet he was a compulsive philanderer, boasting of the number of women he had bedded. He could marvelously evoke, and with economy of words, the smells, the color, and the raucous life of European bars, ports, and cities, yet spent some of his most contented and fruitful years in the United States and chose to end his life in Switzerland "where no one ever rang his doorbell without invitation." He was known as the prolific producer of highly lucrative popular fiction yet his literary reputation is secure. His work has been praised by T. S. Eliot, Somerset Maugham, and Henry Miller, and André Gide described him as "the greatest novelist we have had this century."

Despite his popular success and growing international fame,

Simenon came to believe that his talent was being wasted and in 1934 he told his publisher, Fayard, that he wanted now to concentrate on novels which were psychological studies rather than exercises in ratiocination and which he referred to as *romans durs* or *romans-tout-court*. Among those darker novels, *Les Inconnus dans la maison*, first published in France in 1940, is commonly regarded as one of the most distinguished. Although it was written during the German occupation, the novel does not deal even obliquely with the trauma which France was undergoing. Simenon had decided to continue his working life as normally as possible despite the occupation, and he and others of this view, while being careful not to collaborate or to take any action which was specifically anti-French, did not invite censorship or imprisonment. One of the characters in the novel is a Jew, Justin Luska, whose Jewishness is hardly mentioned. It may be that Simenon was hoping that this subtle sensitivity would be reflected in the film adaptation that followed quite soon after the book's publication, but when the film was released Luska's Jewishness was emphasized and the film was distributed accompanied by a work of crude anti-Semitic propaganda.

Les Inconnus dans la maison was first published in Great Britain as *The Strangers in the House* in 1951. The protagonist in the novel is Hector Loursat de Saint-Marc, a lawyer in the town of Moulins, a man whose family name is highly respected and whose ability as a barrister is acknowledged, but who now is regarded by colleagues and the town people with pity, almost with contempt. For eighteen years since his wife deserted him for another man, leaving him with a two-year-old daughter, he has lived as a drunken recluse, spending most of his life in either his study or the adjoining bedroom with his books and bottles of burgundy. Even the shelves of books, which line his room to the ceiling, provide neither stimulus nor comfort. He seldom enters the other rooms in the house, sees his daughter only at meals, and even then rarely speaks to her. He is as remote from her life as he is from the people of Moulins, from the maid, Angèle, who waits on him at dinner, and the cook, Phine, an ugly wizened woman isolated in her vaulted kitchen, whose hatred of him causes him no concern.

All this changes one October night when he hears the crack of a pistol shot and the sound of running feet. Curious, he makes his way upstairs to a room he hasn't entered for decades, where he discovers an injured man slumped on the bed, one leg swathed in voluminous bandages. Even as Loursat's eyes meet those of the stranger, the man dies. Loursat telephones Rogissart, the public prosecutor whose wife is his cousin, giving the news calmly and succinctly:

> I've just found a stranger in my house...in bed, in one of the rooms on the third floor...He died at the exact moment I reached him...Will you see about it, Gérard? ...It's really tiresome. It looks to me like a criminal affair.

When the prosecutor hangs up, he looks at his wife, who dislikes her cousin and who has been listening through a second earphone. "There he is again! Drunk as usual!" she remarks.

And so the police investigation begins, deputed by the public prosecutor to the examining magistrate, Ducup. Ducup breaks the news to Loursat that while he was self-immured in an alcoholic haze, his daughter Nicole was partying upstairs with a semi-criminal gang of local young people whose secret meeting place is in his house. One of the gang, Emile Manu, the son of a poor widow, has become Nicole's lover, and admits that he was visiting her on the night of the crime. Ducup reports that the rest of the group had filled Manu with drink, then dared him to steal the car belonging to the mayor's secretary and drive them to an inn out of town. Manu ran over and injured a stranger; the gang had taken him to the upstairs room in Loursat's house and had summoned a doctor who could be depended upon to keep their secret. The dead stranger has been identified as a convicted criminal, Louis Gagalin, known as Big Louis. Ducup is able to provide the names of the socially mixed group of young people who were members of the gang. It had been Nicole who had kept her head and suggested bringing the injured man to the house and Phine had been let into the secret. The gang has a strong motive for disposing of this potentially violent and unpleasant guest and Manu is obviously the chief suspect. Despite the prosecutor's wish to keep Nicole's name out of the papers and to deal with this embarrassing case with sensitivity, murder imposes its imperatives; a murdered body cannot be kept secret. Loursat makes his brief statement. He knows nothing of the actions of his daughter, nothing of what has been going on in the house other than in his personal quarters, and regards what happens elsewhere as no concern of his. Having heard an unusual sound like a revolver shot, he made the mistake of concerning himself with the matter and discovered on the second floor a man lying in bed who died a few seconds later of a gunshot wound. He has nothing further to say.

But the discovery of this dead body changes his life. Despising both his legal colleagues and the police, he begins gradually to involve himself in the case and reluctantly, at Manu's request, agrees to become his defending counsel. His daughter, who has remained calm throughout, becomes his assistant. Gradually, almost silently, their relationship develops as they sit night after night assembling material for the defense. Loursat realizes that he actually needs to break out of his stuffy book-lined den whose padded door shuts out all intruding sound, to sit down to dinner with Nicole and tell her simply and casually: "Don't be afraid."

The novel displays the qualities on which Simenon's literary reputation is based: a strong narrative, a setting which is brilliantly and sensitively evoked, a cast in which every character, however minor, is uniquely alive, psychological acuity, and an empathy with the secret lives of apparently ordinary men and women. He writes in a style which combines economy of words with strength and elegance and which has given him a literary reputation rare among novelists in the crime genre. Inevitably, despite the apparent simplicity of style, he is a novelist who loses much in translation.

The Strangers in the House is both a detective story and a psychological investigation of the effect of the murder on all those, particularly Loursat, who come into contact with the crime. The novel is also a brilliant depiction of one kind of alcoholism; not the addiction which results in violence or lachrymose self-pity, but the drink-induced accidie which stultifies both body and spirit. There is no dependence on physical clues in the solution to the mystery of the murdered stranger. Instead Loursat, emerging from his claustrophobic lair, moves again among his colleagues in the criminal justice system and questions the people involved, however marginally, with the death. The reader walks with him, experiencing the changing mood of the little town, participating in the slow system of investigation as Loursat conscientiously carries out his methodical process of recording and interviewing. Simenon is brilliant at selecting the salient facts which bring alive a character or a place, inducing the reader to contribute his own imagination to that of the writer so that more is conveyed than is written.

Although the novel is more a psychological study than a conventional mystery, the tension never slackens and reaches its climax in the last chapter when Loursat harnesses all his neglected forensic skill to save young Emile Manu's life. Longing for the lunchtime adjournment when he would be able to have his two or three glasses of red wine, despising the colleagues around him, the magistrates, the spectators, as "wretched human beings who didn't know why they were alive, who were moved along like cattle," he accepted the reality of what had happened to him with that crack of a pistol shot:

> A gang of young people were discovered, and within twenty-four hours he had left his lair to go scurrying in their wake.
>
> To discover a new world, new people, new sounds and smells, new thoughts, new feelings, a swarming, writhing world, which had no relation to the epics and tragedies of literature, one that was full of all those mysterious and generally trivial details you don't find in books—the breath of cold air in a dirty back alley, the loiterer on a street corner, a shop remaining open long after all others had closed, an impatient, highly strung boy waiting all keyed up outside a watchmaker's for the friend who was going to lead him into a new and unknown future.

It is this mysterious world, these trivial but portentous details and this unknown future, that Simenon, in this novel as in so many others, has made distinctly his own. And Loursat does not change dramatically; Simenon is above all a realist. Loursat still drinks his burgundy, but now sits alone in a little bistro, not in that smoke-filled, book-lined den. And he has received a shiny picture postcard in harsh colors of Vesuvius belching flame and smoke which bears the words "Love from Naples— Nicole and Emile." "Love" was not a word she would have spoken or written to her father in all the twenty years of their shared but severed lives, years in which Loursat, as much as the murdered Gagalin, was a stranger in the house.

—P. D. JAMES

THE STRANGERS IN
THE HOUSE

PART ONE

I

"HELLO! Is that Rogissart?"

The public prosecutor stood shivering in his nightshirt. It certainly was chilly, particularly for his bare feet. He had groped wildly for his slippers while the telephone was ringing, but hadn't been able to find them. Lying in bed, his wife looked at him inquiringly, wondering who could be disturbing them at that hour of the night.

"Who is it?" asked Rogissart.

He frowned at the answer, and for his wife's benefit repeated:

"Loursat?...Oh, it's you, Hector!"

His wife was intrigued. She hoisted herself up onto an elbow, and with the other hand reached for the extension. Hector Loursat, the lawyer, was her first cousin.

"What's the matter?" asked the prosecutor.

At the other end of the line, Loursat answered calmly:

"I've just found a stranger in my house...in bed, in one of the rooms on the third floor...He died at the exact moment I reached him...Will you see about it, Gérard?...It's really tiresome. It looks to me like a criminal affair."

When the prosecutor hung up, he looked at his wife, who couldn't stand her cousin:

"There he is again! Drunk as usual!" she remarked indignantly.

As a matter of fact everything had appeared to be quite in

5

order that evening, all the more so, as the rain falling outside seemed to add to the feeling of stagnation.

It was the first cold rain of the season, and, except for a few couples courting, hardly a soul had gone to the movie on the rue d'Allier. The girl in the box office was in a thoroughly bad temper as she sat freezing in her little glass cage, watching the raindrops falling obliquely through the glare of the street lights.

In other words Moulins was quite itself—the Moulins of any early October day. At the Hôtel de Paris, at the Dauphin, at the Allier, traveling salesmen dined together at the large tables reserved for them, waited on by girls in black dresses, black stockings, and white aprons. Now and then a car drove along the street, making for Nevers or Clermont, or perhaps even for Paris.

The shops were shuttered, their signs glistened with wet—the huge red hat over Buchet's, Tellier's gigantic watch, and the gilded horse's head over the horse butcher's.

The whistling behind the houses was the slow train from Montluçon arriving with barely a dozen passengers.

At the Prefecture a dinner was being given for twenty people. The monthly dinner, as it was called, always gathered together the very same guests.

Hardly a window that was not shuttered. The steps of the rare passerby in the dismal streets sounded furtive, almost embarrassed.

At the corner of a street that housed mostly lawyers and notaries stood the home of the Loursat family, or, to give it its full name, Loursat de Saint-Marc. Though similar in size and style, the structure differed from the other houses in its aloofness. It was remote, sleepy, secret. Between its two wings was a paved courtyard shut off from the street by a high wall. In the middle stood a fountain—an empty basin with a statue of Apollo, from whose mouth protruded a spout through which no water ever came.

In the dining room on the first floor Loursat sat with his round back turned toward the fire, a coal fire that burned with a yellow smoke.

He had pouches under his eyes, but no more than on any other night, and the eyes themselves had a watery look that made them disconcertingly vague.

The round table was laid with a white cloth. Across from Loursat sat his daughter, Nicole, who ate with a sort of mournful earnestness. Neither spoke. Loursat sat hunched over his plate like a grazing animal, chewing noisily and sighing every now and again from boredom or tiredness.

When Loursat had finished his plate, he would push back his chair an inch or two to give his stomach more room. Then he would wait.

He made it so obvious that it had become practically a signal. In response Nicole would turn her head slightly toward the maid, who stood near the door.

The latter would then open what looked like a cupboard, thrust her head inside, and shout down the shaft of the dumbwaiter:

"Next course, please!"

Below, tucked away in her vaulted kitchen, an ugly wizened little creature would get up from her meal, which she was eating at a corner of the huge table. Going over to the stove, she would take a dish from the oven and put it into the dumbwaiter.

Almost invariably the latter jammed after rising only a few feet, and there was nothing for it but to haul it down and start afresh. That had to be done several times before, by a lucky chance, the thing went jerkily up to its destination.

The fire didn't draw properly. The house was full of things that either wouldn't work at all or worked badly. Everybody noticed them. Elbows on the table, Loursat heaved a sigh each time the dumbwaiter stalled; and again whenever a gust of

7

wind blew a whirl of smoke into the room. Nicole showed her annoyance by drumming on the table with her fingers.

"Well, Angèle? . . . What is it?"

Nicole helped herself from a carafe of white wine. Her father had a bottle of burgundy, which he managed to polish off unaided over the course of the meal.

"I was going to ask you, Mademoiselle . . . would you please let me have my wages as soon as dinner's over?"

Loursat listened, though without paying much attention. He hardly knew the maid in question, a more vigorous-looking girl than most of the others they had had, in fact a strapping, raw-boned lass whose manner, if not openly rude, was devoid of all respect.

"Have you got your keys?"

"I have given them to Phine."

Phine was Joséphine, the undersized creature in the lower regions who sent up the dishes.

"All right."

Loursat didn't ask his daughter why the maid was leaving. He didn't know which of them had given the other notice. A new maid usually lasted only a fortnight, and Loursat didn't care.

He ate the boiled chestnuts, and managed in the process to spill plenty onto his black velveteen smoking jacket. That didn't matter either, for the jacket was in any case covered with grease spots. From somewhere or other came the sound of trickling water, which no doubt meant a leaking tap—yet another thing in need of repair.

Having finished his chestnuts, Loursat waited a moment to see if there was anything more to come, then crumpled up his napkin into a ball and put it on the table, for he could never be bothered to fold it properly. He got up.

It was just the same every evening, without the slightest variation. Loursat didn't look at Nicole. Only, as he made for the door, he grunted:

"Goodnight."

His step was already heavy, and his gait, if not exactly stumbling, was uncertain. After all, since the morning, he'd drunk two or three bottles of burgundy, more likely three than two, which he brought up from the cellar first thing, and handled with great care.

His course through the house could have been followed from outside as the lights in the passages went on and off, showing through the slats of the shutters. The last light, which was not switched off, came from his study, the last room in the right wing.

The door was padded. It always had been, at any rate in the days of Loursat's father, who had been a lawyer too, and very likely in the days of his grandfather, who had been mayor of the town for something like twenty years. The black material was torn in one or two places, revealing the wadding beneath.

There was a marble mantelpiece, its dignity somewhat impaired by the common little cast-iron stove with an elbowed stove-pipe that at some period or other had been installed temporarily and then allowed to remain. It was certainly a much more businesslike affair than the grate it had replaced. It burned with a roar and in no time became red hot. Loursat tended it as affectionately as if it had been a faithful dog, throwing the odd shovelful of charcoal into its maw, then crouching dawn to poke the embers.

The slow train from Montluçon had come and gone. Screams from another train floated over the town, but that was only a freight train. An old film flickered on the screen in front of a few handfuls of people scattered about in the cinema, which smelled of wet clothes. The chief of police had ushered his guests into the smoking room and was handing around the cigars.

There being no bridge that evening, Rogissart, the public prosecutor, had taken the opportunity to go to bed early, where he and his wife lay side by side, reading.

Loursat blew his nose as old men and peasants do, opening his handkerchief out to the full, blowing three, four, or even five trumpet-like blasts, then carefully folding it up again.

He was all alone in his overheated den, where he had locked himself in. Nicole used to say that was a vice, but it was really just a matter of taste.

His gray hair was naturally shaggy and he increased its untidiness by constantly running his fingers through it. His untrimmed beard was more or less pointed, his moustache was stained yellow from smoking.

There were cigarette ends everywhere. The ashtrays were overflowing, and they were on the floor, the mantelpiece, on books, and among papers.

For a while Loursat sat at his desk, smoking, then got up heavily and went over to the stove to fetch a bottle that stood beside it, warming.

A few blocks off, cars splashed along the rue de Paris, with their windshield wipers going, their headlights lighting up the raindrops; the faces inside were pale.

Loursat did nothing. He let his cigarette go out, lit it again, and, when it was finished, just threw the butt on the floor.

He picked up a book, opened it at random, and started reading, sipping his wine from time to time, crossing and uncrossing his legs.

The room was full of books, shelves and shelves of them right up to the ceiling. Indeed there were far more in the house than that room alone could contain. They had long ago overflowed into the passages and found their way into most of the other rooms of the house. Some of them were his, others had come down to him from his father or his grandfather.

Sometimes he would trudge off to the other end of the house, and there stand gazing dejectedly at a row of books, apparently quite forgetting what he had come for. He might smoke his cigarette right to the end, before finally reaching out almost reluctantly for a volume and carrying it off to his own lair.

It had been going on for twenty years—no, eighteen to be exact—and never once in all that time had anyone ever persuaded him to dine out, neither the Rogissarts, who were cousins and who had friends in for dinner and bridge every Friday, nor the senior member of the bar, who had been an intimate friend of his father's, nor Dossin, his brother-in-law, whose house was frequented by politicians. Not even the successive chiefs of police, though each in turn, new to the town and its personalities, had persisted for a while in sending him invitations.

He scratched his head, grunted, snorted, coughed, blew his nose, spat. He was hot. His waistcoat was covered by cigarette ash. He read ten pages of a treatise on jurisprudence—for after all he was a lawyer—then threw it down and plunged into the middle of some seventeenth-century memoirs.

As the hours slipped by, he seemed to become more ponderous, his eyes acquired a faraway look, and his movements a hieratic slowness.

The principal bedroom, always referred to as *the bedroom*, the room that had always been occupied by the masters and mistresses of the house, and which he too had once occupied with his wife, was in the other wing of the house. But it was many years since Loursat had slept there. When his bottle was empty, sometimes at midnight, sometimes in the small hours of the morning, he got to his feet, opened the window an inch or two to get rid of any fumes from the stove, and he never forgot, as he left the room, to turn out the light.

He slept in the adjoining room, which he could reach directly by a communicating door. It had formerly been a secretary's office, but had since been provided with a simple iron bedstead. There he would undress, leaving the door open, and clamber into bed, where he went on smoking until he heaved a sigh and settled down to sleep.

That evening—it must have been the second Wednesday of the month since it was the day of the monthly dinner at the Prefecture—that evening Loursat stoked up his stove with special care, as the cold and the wet outside made the misty atmosphere indoors all the more luxurious.

He could hear the patter of the rain and now and again the creaking hinge of a shutter that hadn't been properly closed and was caught by one of the sudden gusts of wind that swept along the street. He could also hear, insistent as a metronome, the ticking of his watch in his waistcoat pocket.

He had for the last hour or so been reading a life of Tamerlane in an old edition that had a moldy smell and a binding that was crumbling away. He had put the book down. Perhaps he was thinking of fetching another, but, if he was, the idea was banished from his mind. He raised his head slowly, surprised, interested.

Normally few sounds reached him in his study. There was Joséphine, of course, who slept in a room immediately above. She went upstairs at exactly ten o'clock every night, and stumped about overhead for a good half hour before finally getting into bed.

But Phine had got into bed at least an hour ago. The sound he had just heard was quite an unusual one, in fact it was precisely its strangeness that had roused Loursat from his torpor.

At first he thought of the crack of a whip, a common enough sound to hear in the early morning when the garbagemen went on their rounds.

But this noise hadn't come from outside. Nor was it the crack of a whip. There was more weight in it than that, more percussion, so much so that he had felt a slight shock in his chest before his ears actually heard it.

As he looked up, listening, the expression on his face was one of slight annoyance at the intrusion. It might have been taken for anxiety, but it wasn't that.

What was so impressive was the silence that followed. A silence more compact, more positive than any ordinary one, but which yet seemed full of strained vibrations.

He didn't get up from his chair at once. He filled his glass, emptied it, put his cigarette back in his mouth, then heaved himself up and went over to the door, where he listened for a second before opening it.

When he switched on the light in the passage, three dusty lamps lit up receding stretches of emptiness. There was no one there, nothing except that weighty, tense silence.

"Nicole!" he called softly.

He was certain now that it was a shot that he had heard. He still tried to persuade himself that it might have come from outside, but he didn't really believe it.

He didn't get excited. On the contrary he walked slowly and heavily, his round back making him look rather like a bear. According to his cousin, Mme Rogissart, he adopted that appearance on purpose, to impress people. But then, she always had plenty to say about him, and precious little of it was ever good.

He went along the passage to the center of the house. Reaching the top of the white stone staircase, he leant over the handsome forged-iron banisters and gazed down into the empty hall below.

"Nicole!"

Once again he had hardly raised his voice, yet it seemed to echo throughout the house.

Should he give it up and go back to the warmth and peacefulness he had just left?

A faint sound reached him from the floor above, the sound of a sneaking footstep. No one lived up there, not in that part of the third floor, though no doubt every attic had been occupied in the old days when the household had included a butler, a coachman, a gardener, and maids.

Nicole slept in a room at the far end of the left wing, and her father started off along a passage similar to the one that had led him from his own quarters, except that one of the bulbs had gone of the three lamps that hung from the ceiling. He stopped at a door. Had there been a glint of light under it? Loursat thought so, but it was instantly switched off.

"Nicole!" he called once again.

He knocked on the door. His daughter's voice answered:

"Who is it?"

He could have sworn the sound didn't come from where the bed was—to the left of the door. At any rate that was where it had been the last time he had been into the room, though admittedly that had been at least two years before.

"Let me in," he said simply.

"Just a moment."

There was a very long pause. On the other side of the door someone was going to and fro while trying to make as little noise as possible.

At the end of the passage were the back stairs leading, on the one hand, up to the attics, on the other, down to the kitchen and pantries.

Loursat was still standing there when one of these stairs creaked. There was no possible doubt about it. And, when he turned around as quickly as possible, he felt absolutely certain he saw something, though it was the merest glimpse of a disappearing figure. Someone had nipped past and down the stairs, and it was a man rather than a woman. Yes, definitely a man, probably a young man, and dressed in a beige mackintosh.

The door opened and Nicole stood facing her father. She looked at him calmly. On her features was no trace either of curiosity or of affection. She seemed quite indifferent.

"What do you want?"

The light that hung from the ceiling was on. So was her bedside lamp. The sheets were in disarray but Loursat thought they had been rumpled deliberately. As for Nicole, she was in her dressing-gown, but beneath it he noticed she still had on her stockings.

"Didn't you hear anything?" he asked, glancing once more toward the back stairs.

For some reason or other she found it necessary to lie.

"I was asleep," she answered.

"There's someone in the house."

"Really?"

Nicole's clothes lay scattered on the carpet.

"I even thought I heard a shot."

He went to the end of the passage. He wasn't afraid. He had a good mind to shrug his shoulders and go back to his own room. But if there had been a shot, if he really had seen a man on the stairs, it was worth going to have a look.

To his surprise Nicole didn't follow him at once. She remained behind in her room, and a few seconds later, when she caught up with him, she had removed her stockings.

Not that he minded. She could do just as she liked. But he couldn't help noticing.

"I'm sure a man came down these stairs. Since we haven't heard a door open and shut, he's presumably still in the house. Perhaps he's hiding somewhere."

"I can't think why a burglar should want to come to this house . . . unless he was interested in old books."

Nicole was taller than her father, her figure full and even a little plump. She had a mass of fair hair with a reddish tinge in it, a tinge that had also worked its way into her warm brown eyes, which were set off by a milky complexion.

She followed him resignedly. She wasn't afraid either. Merely a bit put out.

"I can't hear a sound," he said, pausing at the bottom of the stairs.

It occurred to him that his daughter might have been receiving a young man in her room, a thought that once more tempted him to go back to his room, for that certainly was no concern of his.

By chance he looked up and saw that the landing at the top of the stairs was faintly lit up by a light that must be burning somewhere up on the third floor.

"There's a light on up there."

"Perhaps it's Phine."

He looked at her contemptuously. What would Phine be doing at that time of night in the opposite wing to where her own room was, a wing that was never used unless it was for lumber? Besides, Phine was notoriously scared of the least thing and was the last person to be wandering about when others had gone to bed. So nervous was she that whenever Loursat went away for a few days, she insisted on moving her bed into Nicole's room.

Slowly and heavily he went up the stairs. He knew he was annoying Nicole by his insistence. This was the first time in years that he had departed from his own narrow and strictly prescribed orbit.

They were penetrating into an almost unknown world as they climbed the last flight of stairs. Loursat sniffed. At each step he became more convinced there was a faint smell of gunpowder.

The passage up here was narrower. On the floor was a threadbare strip of carpet that had served its better years on the floor below, where it had been replaced at least thirty years ago. Both walls were covered with shelves, and here too were books, thousands of them, paperbacks, reviews, and even stacks of old newspapers.

Nicole was still following, unperturbed.

"You see! There's no one here."

She didn't add, "You've been drinking again!" But the tone of her voice suggested it plainly.

"All the same, somebody switched that light on," he sighed, pointing to the unshaded bulb that lit up the passage.

"And smoked this cigarette," he added stooping down to pick up the burned end, which was still warm.

He was out of breath from having climbed so many stairs. He went on rather halfheartedly. He was still inclined to think he'd do much better to mind his own business.

His memories of this part of the house were almost all those of childhood. The room they were just passing on the left had belonged to Eva, a housemaid, for whom he had long nursed a secret passion. Then one day he had found her with the chauffeur in a position he had never forgotten.

Two doors further on was the room that had belonged to Eusèbe, the gardener. It was Eusèbe who had taught him how to snare sparrows.

The door wasn't quite shut, but it wasn't for that reason that Loursat pushed it open. He was merely mildly curious to see what had become of Eusèbe's room. Nicole hung back.

It was dark inside, but there was no longer the slightest doubt about the smell of gunpowder, mixed though it was with that of tobacco smoke. Besides there was a faint sound of someone moving.

For a second or two he groped for the switch, then suddenly the room was flooded with light and Loursat found himself confronted by two eyes that stared at him.

He didn't move. He couldn't. It was altogether too extraordinary, not merely the situation, but still more the expression in those eyes.

They were those of a person lying in bed, whose body was

only partly concealed by bedclothes. One leg hung down over the side of the bed, and it was swathed in such voluminous bandages as to suggest a limb in a splint.

Loursat, however, hardly took in those details. What absorbed his attention were those eyes that gazed back at him full of an immense bewilderment.

The body and the thick, crew-cut hair were those of a man. But the eyes were those of a child, big frightened eyes that seemed to be hesitating on the verge of tears.

The nose quivered, the lips twitched. A grimace that again suggested tears. Or was he attempting to cry out?

A noise...a human voice...something between a gurgle and the wail of a newborn infant...

Then he slumped back into the bed, became motionless. It had happened so suddenly that it took Loursat's breath away.

When he recovered his self-possession, he ran his fingers through his hair and in a voice that sounded to him as though it came from somewhere else he managed to say, "He must be dead."

He turned toward Nicole, who was standing further down the landing, her unstockinged feet shoved into a pair of sky-blue slippers. He said it again: "He must be dead."

And then, more naturally: "Who is he?"

He wasn't drunk. As a matter of fact he never was, whatever people might say. As the day wore on, his whole being seemed to become rather more ponderous, his head especially, and his thoughts lost their outline. They were strung together by a thread that was not that of everyday logic. Sometimes he would come out with a few words grunted under his breath, the only indications of what was going on inside his head.

Nicole gazed at him in a sort of stupor, as though the extraordinary thing that night was not the revolver shot, the lamp left burning on the second floor, the stranger dying in that bed, but this man, her father, who stood there before her calm and weighty.

The girl at the theater entrance had at last been able to lock up the little box office, which, despite hot-water foot warmers, was a torture to her all through the winter. The last couples were leaving, pausing for an instant under the bright lights, then plunging into the darkness and the rain. Soon, in various parts of the town, front doors would open and shut again after a loudly whispered:

"Goodnight."

"See you tomorrow."

At the Prefecture, glasses of orangeade were handed around, the first signal that it was time for people to go.

"Hello! Rogissart here."

The public prosecutor stood shivering in his nightshirt. He had never been able to get used to pajamas, though he had tried more than once. He frowned and looked at his wife, who raised her eyes from her book.

"What's that you say?"

Loursat was back in his own room. Nicole, still in her dressing gown, stood near the door. Phine hadn't put in an appearance. If she was awake, she was no doubt lying petrified by fear, very likely with her head under the bedclothes, trying not to hear anything yet at the same time listening intently.

When he rang off, Loursat wanted to pour himself a drink, but the bottle was empty. He'd already consumed his quota. If he wanted another he'd have to go and fetch it, which meant first lighting a candle, as he'd never made up his mind to have electricity installed in the cellars.

"I think you'll be questioned," he said to his daughter. "You'd better think over what you're going to say. Perhaps it would be as well to get dressed."

She looked back at him forbiddingly. That was only natural, as it had always been understood that there was no place in that house for affection. They were never rude to each other, but then they never had occasion to be, as they practically never exchanged a word.

"If you know the man, it would perhaps be wisest to say so straightaway. As for the man I saw going downstairs—"

She repeated what she had already told him:

"I know nothing whatever about it."

"Just as you like. No doubt Phine will be questioned too, and that girl—what's her name—Angèle."

He didn't look at her. He nevertheless had the impression his words went home.

"It won't be long before they're here," he said finally, getting to his feet and making for the door.

It would be an interminable business, he knew well. Rogissart wouldn't come alone. He would certainly bring his clerk and a police inspector, and the latter would doubtless bring one or two of his minions. If refreshments had to be offered, there were plenty of spirits and liqueurs handy in a cupboard. But they wouldn't do for Loursat. He never touched them.

He wandered off in search of a candle. He found one in the kitchen after a lot of searching, for he was like a stranger in his own house, and was only familiar with his own sector. Not like when Eva was still here.

Finally he found what he wanted, went down to the cellar, and returned, panting, with a fresh bottle of burgundy.

On his way up he paused on the ground floor to examine the back door, which opened onto a little blind alley, l'impasse des Tanneurs.

The door was unlocked. He opened it, but shut it again

quickly, repelled by the cold night air and an unpleasant smell of dustbins.

When he got back to his study, Nicole had disappeared. She must have gone to get dressed. He heard a noise in the street, opened a shutter a few inches, and peered out. It was a policeman on a bicycle; Rogissart must have sent him on in advance.

Loursat carefully broke the sealing wax over the cork and drew out the latter. If he seemed intent on what he was doing, his mind still dwelled nevertheless on the dead man upstairs.

He had been shot in the chest at close range by someone who appeared to have been anything but calm and collected, for the bullet, which no doubt had been intended for the heart, had entered the body only just below the neck. No doubt that was why the wounded man, instead of uttering a cry, was only able to produce that queer gurgling sound. He had died from loss of blood.

He was a huge creature, looking somehow all the more enormous as a lifeless mass. Standing up, he would have been a head taller than Loursat, to say the least of it. His features were coarse, those of a peasant, of a robust unthinking brute.

Loursat sipped his wine.

"Funny," he muttered.

Which, after all, was a funny word to use!

He heard a sound overhead. That would be Phine turning over. It didn't mean she was getting up. Not at all. She wouldn't venture from that bed of hers unless she was dragged from it.

At the Hôtel de Paris three salesmen were playing *belote* with the proprietor, who glanced occasionally at the clock. The cafés were shutting. At the Prefecture too, the concierge shut the big doors that enclosed the inner courtyard after the last car had driven off.

It was raining harder than ever, coming down in slanting streaks, driven by the northwest wind, which must have been blowing up a storm out at sea.

His elbows on his desk, Loursat scratched his head, letting his cigarette ash drop onto the lapel of his jacket. His big glaucous eyes wandered around the room as, with a sigh, he murmured:

"This'll give them a jolt!"

Them—that meant everybody, and first of all Rogissart or, rather, his wife, Laurence, who was even more concerned with such matters than he was; concerned, that is to say, with all questions of right and wrong, with what was done, and, still more, with what was the done thing.

The others too, the people in the Palais de Justice, for instance, who didn't know which way to look on those rare occasions when Loursat appeared in court, the magistrates, the lawyers, the court clerk, and everyone else.

The people like Dossin, his brother-in-law, who manufactured the Dossin threshing machine and who tried to worm his way into the good graces of politicians with the hope of one day becoming a *conseiller général*; his wife, Marthe, who draped herself in flimsy clothing and played the part of a plaintive invalid. She was Loursat's only sister, yet they hadn't seen each other for years.

Still others—in fact the whole lot of them—his neighbors and all the pillars of propriety, the people who were either men of means or pretended to be, the shopkeepers and hotel owners, the members of the Syndicat d'Initiative, all of them great and small right down to the ragtag and bobtail.

They'd have to start an investigation.

Because a stranger had been found dying in one of the rooms upstairs.

In the house of a Loursat de Saint-Marc!

For in a roundabout and somewhat mystical way he was related to the whole town. Had not the latter lain for well-nigh twenty years under the paternal rule of his grandfather, who now had a street named after him and a statue standing in the middle of a square?

He finished off his glass and poured himself another, from which he had taken no more than a sip when two cars drew up in front of the house.

Phine was still in bed, and Nicole had not reappeared, so there was nothing for it but to go down and open the front door himself.

He ambled down and started fiddling with the unfamiliar locks, while from outside came the sound of car doors opening and closing.

2

IT WAS eleven o'clock when he opened his eyes, but he didn't know it, not yet, for he couldn't be bothered to reach out for his watch, which was still in his waistcoat pocket. The room was as dim as a cellar—the only light that could enter had to zigzag past the slats of the shutters, except in two places, two small round holes that shone brightly.

It was those two bright spots that Loursat studied gravely, with just that gravity, in fact, that children bestow on trifles. The thing was to guess from them what sort of day it was outside. It could hardly be said that Loursat was superstitious. Nonetheless he had his little fads and fancies. This was one of them. He had to guess, and, if he guessed right, it was a good omen.

He made up his mind: it was sunny! Then he turned over heavily and reached for the electric bell, which let loose a startling din in Phine's sepulchral kitchen.

She was there, pouring out a glass of wine to a uniformed policeman who sat at the table making himself very much at home.

"What's that?" he asked.

"Nothing to worry about," she answered disdainfully.

With his eyes open, the lawyer lay on his back waiting, listening to the sounds in the house. They were too far away and confused, however, for him to be able to identify them. He rang again. The policeman looked inquiringly at Phine, who shrugged her shoulders.

"If only he'd die!"

She took up a coffeepot that was standing on the side of the stove, poured off its contents into a smaller one, and put the latter on a tray, where she also collected a few other items including a bowl of fly-blown sugar, which had been sitting on the table.

Upstairs she didn't trouble to knock or to say good morning. She simply put the tray down on the chair that served as a bed-side table, then went over to the window and threw open the shutters.

The result was disappointing. Loursat thought for a moment he had lost, for the sky was overcast, the color of mercury. The next moment, however, it had cleared sufficiently to let through an ephemeral sunbeam, which then made haste to vanish as rainclouds scudded across in the icy wind.

"Is there anybody downstairs?"

This was a difficult time of the day. It generally lasted an hour or so, during which he took every precaution. Every movement had to be slow and calculated, particularly if it was his head. A jerk of the head was very unpleasant indeed. His stomach, too, was easily upset.

Sipping his coffee, he listened to Phine lighting the study fire, a job she attacked with such violence that you'd have thought she had a grudge against the stove.

"There are people downstairs, and people upstairs. In fact they're all over the house."

"And Mademoiselle?"

"She's been shut up with one of them in the main drawing room for the last hour."

Phine's moods might well have been treated as a joke. If they weren't, it was because the others were used to them. She'd been there too long. Nicole had been only two years old when Phine had virtually taken her in charge. From that time onward, she had displayed nothing but hatred toward everyone else, especially Loursat.

He didn't interfere. He made it a principle to shut his eyes to all that went on in the house. Once or twice, however, quite unintentionally, on opening a door he had surprised Phine on her knees warming the little girl's bare feet with her hands or by pressing them against her dried-up breasts.

After that, as though to disprove her capacity for tenderness, she would be as disagreeable as possible to everybody, Nicole included.

Having finished his coffee, Loursat lay still for a quarter of an hour, when it was time for the bottle of mineral water. He drank the whole bottle, gargling the stuff before swallowing it. Only then could he get up and dress, though care had still to be exercised in every movement. It wasn't till something like an hour later, after his second or third glass of burgundy, that he really felt himself.

"Has Rogissart been again?"

"I couldn't tell. I don't know him."

He rarely used the bathroom. It was too far away, right over in the other wing. He did perfectly well with the sort of washstand that had been improvised on the shelf of a cupboard. He got dressed in front of Phine as she struggled with the stove, which she never managed to light on the first attempt.

"How's Mademoiselle this morning?"

To which the other snapped:

"How do you expect her to be?"

It had been rather a comic performance the night before, when you came to think about it.

The public prosecutor was very tall and thin. Just like his wife. Indeed they were sometimes disrespectfully referred to as the two scarecrows.

He had looked worried as he shook his cousin's hand and he had asked, frowning, "What was it you were trying to tell me over the telephone?"

Obviously he wouldn't have been at all surprised if Hector Loursat had answered with a grin, "Go on! I was only pulling your leg!"

Nothing of the sort. There was a dead body in the house all right, and it was almost as if Loursat were happy to show it off.

"There you are," he said. "I don't know who it is or how he got here. As a matter of fact I haven't tried to find out. That's really your job, isn't it?"

Rogissart's clerk coughed every other moment, till in the end he got on everybody's nerves. There was also an inspector of the Brigade Mobile, a man called Binet or Linet or something of the sort, a short man with thinning hair and fish-like eyes who seemed to be constantly apologizing for something or other. He too was irritating. He was always in the way, and his chocolate-colored overcoat was somehow rather offensive.

"Is Nicole in the house?" asked Rogissart with the air of a man performing a very disagreeable duty.

"She's dressing. She'll be here in a moment."

"Does she know?"

"She was with me when I opened the door."

Loursat had certainly drunk quite a lot—rather more than usual—and there was just a slight thickness in his speech. That alone was embarrassing enough—not for Loursat but for the prosecutor—in the presence of the clerk and the police inspector, and two other men who had just joined them.

"Do you mean to say nobody in the house knows this man?"

Nicole was splendid. Right from the start. Her entry couldn't have been better if she'd rehearsed it for a week. It was surprising to everybody, including her father, to see her such a woman of the world. She was like a hostess entering the drawing-room where her guests have been waiting for her.

She made straight for the prosecutor, holding out her hand.

"Good evening, Cousin."

Then she turned toward the others as though expecting to be introduced, "Messieurs."

It was quite a revelation. She had never been like that before.

"Suppose we go somewhere else," suggested Rogissart, ill at ease in the presence of that corpse with wide-open eyes. "I expect you'd like to stay, Inspector, and have a look around..."

They went down to the dining room, the only room available apart from Loursat's study. The drawing room hadn't been used for many years.

"Do you mind if I ask Nicole some questions, Hector?"

"Go ahead. I'll leave you to it. If you want me, I'll be in my study."

Half an hour later Rogissart joined him there. He came alone.

"She assures me she knows absolutely nothing about it. You know, Hector, this is really a very serious matter. I've given orders for the body to be taken to the mortuary. I can't very well open an inquiry in the middle of the night—not officially. We'll start that in the morning. Meanwhile I'm afraid I'll have to leave a man in the house."

Of course! He could leave half a dozen for all Loursat cared!

"You've really no idea what's been going on?"

"Not the slightest!"

The answer was given in such an offhand manner that Rogissart was more disconcerted than ever. Was his cousin refusing to be helpful? Or was he treating the whole thing as a joke?

Obviously it was going to be a very ticklish affair. It needed very special handling. For, if the man was a drunkard and an impossible creature in every way, he was nonetheless a Loursat de Saint-Marc.

He never went out. He never mixed in society. He nonetheless belonged to it.

And his being a recluse to some extent mitigated his principal failing. He drank, but he did so privately in his own home without causing a scandal.

Indeed, though he was often judged severely, he was still more often pitied.

"It's a shame! Such an able man! He could have done so much! When he gets going, there's no one in town who can touch him."

It was true, as he showed once or twice in the course of a year, when he took his place at the bar.

No one had guessed what would happen when his wife had suddenly left him eighteen years ago, a few days before Christmas, leaving him alone with his two-year-old baby. During the weeks that followed many people had called at the house, only to find the door obstinately closed to them.

Finally his cousin, Rogissart, who had one day successfully buttonholed him, took him to task about it.

"Come on, old man! You really mustn't let yourself go. You can't spend the rest of your life as a hermit!"

Couldn't he? He proceeded to prove that he could, and he had kept it up for eighteen years, eighteen years during which he had needed neither a wife, nor a mistress, nor a friend. He was self-sufficient. Even from the domestics he demanded the barest minimum. Phine, whom he had taken on, mainly concerned herself with looking after Nicole.

He simply washed his hands of Nicole. He didn't hate her, for he couldn't allow such a passion as hatred to intrude upon his solitude. He banished her from his life, not merely because he had shrunk in upon himself, but because he shrewdly suspected her of being in fact the child of another man, a man who had formerly held a post in the Prefecture.

This undramatic catastrophe had impressed everybody partly because it had been so completely unexpected. There had been no scandal to lead up to it, nor for that matter any in the sequel. No one even knew what became of the woman.

She was called Geneviève. She came from one of the ten top families of the town. She was pretty and delicately made, and when she married everyone said it was a real love match.

No breath of scandal for three years, not even a catty insinuation. And the next thing they knew was that she had gone off with Bernard, without a word. It was discovered that they'd been having an affair for ages, and according to some it had started even before her marriage.

No one knew what became of them. Her parents, it's true, did once get a picture postcard from Egypt, but it gave no address and they heard no more.

His mouth was still thick as he trudged along the passage landing to the main staircase. There, looking down, he saw a couple of men sitting on the bottom stair. He gazed at them for a moment with the peculiar stare he had acquired in the course of years, a stare at the same time vague and heavy that was impossible to interpret and for that reason troubling to the person stared at. Then he labored up to the third floor, where he could hear sounds of activity.

He entered the room where the man had been killed just as Inspector Binet—for that turned out to be his name—took three steps backward, presumably to get a better view of something. He bumped into the newcomer, to whom he poured out a torrent of profuse apologies.

There were three other men with him, one of them a photographer with a huge camera mounted on a tripod. They went on with their work, with cigarettes in their mouths, measuring distances, moving furniture, hunting in every corner.

"Has the prosecutor been here this morning?" asked the lawyer after quietly surveying the scene.

"No. I don't think he's coming. The examining magistrate's downstairs. The case has been handed over to him."

"Which one?"

"Monsieur Ducup. I think he's downstairs questioning somebody now...I hope you'll excuse us..."

"What for?"

"For—for turning your house upside down."

Loursat went off, shrugging his shoulders. It was time for him to go down to the cellar to fetch his daily ration of burgundy.

The house was cold, full of unwelcome drafts and unusual noises. It was strange to walk about your own house and meet someone you didn't know at every corner, someone who'd walk straight past you, going about his business as though the place belonged to him. If the doorbell rang, it was a policeman who'd go and answer it.

No doubt the servants in the neighboring houses spent half the morning peering out of their front doors or leaning out of windows to see what was going on. A few minutes later the lawyer came panting up from the lower regions. With a bottle in one hand and two in the other he wandered past the policemen without the remotest concern for what they might be thinking.

As he passed the main drawing room, the door opened and Nicole came out. She held herself very erect and rather stiffly, but her composure this time was just a little overdone. Instinctively she stopped on seeing her father. Behind her he could see Ducup, in his best bib and tucker, on whose lips floated the perpetual sarcastic smile with which he kept at bay any possible infringement on his dignity.

The smile grew a shade more sarcastic at the sight of Loursat's bottles. Nicole looked at them too. For a moment she seemed on the point of saying something, but changing her mind, she moved off without a word.

"*Mon cher maître*," began Ducup.

He was a young man of thirty with hair slicked down over a head that made one think of a devitalized rat. If he was ill-favored physically, however, he had pull. He had got on quickly and was going to go a lot further before he'd finished. He'd taken the necessary steps. He had married a girl with a squint, but who was related to some of the most influential families in the locality.

"*Mon cher maître*, they told me you were still asleep and I didn't wish to disturb you."

Loursat walked calmly into the room and put his bottles down on a table, one that must have been brought specially for the examining magistrate, since it wasn't there usually.

The room was vast and almost bare, there being little furniture apart from the gilt chairs that lined the walls, as though for a dance. The parquet floor had not been swept for some time and it was years since it had been polished. The shutters of only one window had been thrown open, and as there was no fire Ducup had kept on his overcoat. The examining magistrate's clerk, sitting with a pile of papers in front of him, got up hastily as Loursat entered. With each step he took, the vast crystal chandelier tinkled musically.

"Monsieur le Procureur has entrusted the case to me, and I have started off by questioning your daughter."

On one point Loursat was quite definite: he didn't want to be interrogated in that huge, cold room. He gave a hasty look around as though looking for some possible corner in which they could stow themselves away cozily—though what he really needed more than anything was a corkscrew and a glass—then grunted curtly, "Come to my room."

And, picking up his bottles, he led the way.

The clerk wondered whether he was supposed to follow, and Ducup was at a loss himself to know what he ought to decide. It was Loursat who settled the question for him. Turning to the clerk he said in a tone of the utmost finality, "We'll send for you when we want you."

He hadn't yet lit the cigarette he'd had in his mouth for the last half hour and which was beginning to come unstuck.

He went upstairs, the examining magistrate after him. In his study he kicked the door shut, then put down his bottles again. Here in his own den he began to feel more like his real self. He sniffed, he snorted, he blew his nose. Then he drew the cork from one of the bottles and poured himself a glass of wine. Holding the bottle up, he turned to his companion.

"What about you?"

"Never at this time of the morning, thanks...I've had a long talk with your daughter. We've been at it for the last two hours. In the end I succeeded in convincing her that she'd be making a great mistake if she didn't tell me what she knew..."

Loursat had been fidgeting about in his chair like a cat who turns around and around before finally settling down. At last he found the right position, in which he could poke the fire with one hand and refill his glass with the other.

"I don't need to tell you, *mon cher maître*, that when the prosecutor did me the honor this morning of—"

It was uphill work with Loursat, who didn't seem to be listening, but whose eyes said plainly: "Idiot!"

"It was only under pressure that I accepted, and—"

"A cigarette?"

"No thank you...It was obvious from the first that if a man was found upstairs in bed someone in the house must know something about him. Starting with that idea, I had to choose between—"

"Look here, Ducup! Suppose you tell me straight out what my daughter told you."

"I was coming to that. I confess I had a job to drag it out of her, but I couldn't help respecting her reticence since it was prompted by a reluctance to betray certain friendships..."

"You're beginning to get on my nerves, Ducup!"

As a matter of fact, he didn't really say "nerves" but a much ruder word. With that he wriggled himself a little deeper in his chair. What with the stove on the one hand and the wine on the other, he was beginning to warm up.

"You'll understand my embarrassment later," Ducup went on. "It's the same old story. We take appearances for reality, little suspecting that the truth behind them is really quite otherwise, that beneath the surface lies a—"

Loursat had his handkerchief to his nose and blew a series of trumpet blasts. He did it deliberately to cut the magistrate's observations short.

Ducup stiffened visibly.

"Very well, then! You may as well know that Mademoiselle Nicole has been going out at night with friends. On other nights she's had her friends here."

He paused, waiting for his revelation to have its effect. Far from wincing, however, Loursat appeared delighted with the news.

"Where?" he asked. "In her room?"

"Upstairs, in a sort of lumber room on the third floor which they christened the 'mess.'"

The telephone rang. Loursat never answered it at once. He rather resented its insistence, though he always had to give in to it in the end.

"Who is it?...Oh it's you, Rogissart...Yes...He's here with me now...No. I don't know anything yet. He doesn't get to the point very quickly...You'd like to speak to him? Right. Hold on..."

With almost trembling eagerness Ducup seized the receiver.

"Yes, Monsieur le Procureur...But of course, Monsieur le Procureur..."

A pause. A glance at Loursat.

"Yes. I was just telling him...I beg your pardon?...very well, Monsieur le Procureur...I was just telling him that a group of young people of the town, among whom was Mademoiselle Nicole, have been in the habit of meeting in the evenings, sometimes in a bar near the marketplace, sometimes...er... under this roof!...Yes, Monsieur le Procureur, in a room up on the third floor...No, not that room. Another one...Two weeks ago a new person joined the group...By way of a joke, they filled him up with drink, then dared him to steal a car and drive them all off to an inn ten kilometers outside the town..."

Another glance at Loursat.

"Yes, I've taken the names...Just so! I thought of that at once...It was undoubtedly that car belonging to the mayor's secretary, which the police found next day with a battered bumper with bloodstains on it...What?...Excuse me, Monsieur le Procureur...Yes, I've got the list in front of me."

If only Loursat would keep still! What possessed him to get up and wander around and around the room? No other conceivable motive but to distract the magistrate's attention and make him nervous. Ducup threw him glances that at first were impatient and finally beseeching, but Loursat ambled on and on, around and around, puffing and blowing.

"Here they are, Monsieur le Procureur...First of all Edmond Dossin...Yes, the son of Charles Dossin...I beg your pardon?...I can't be sure about that. It's difficult to get any precise information as to which of them did what...Then there's Jules Daillat, whose father keeps that pork butcher's shop in the rue d'Allier...That's right, I was intending to look into that. For the moment I've no more than the names. Next comes Destrivaux. I haven't got his Christian name. A bank clerk. Works at the Crédit du Centre where his father is cashier ...Hello! Are you there, Monsieur le Procureur?... Lastly a fellow called Luska. That completed the group until the arrival of a newcomer called Emile Manu. His mother's a widow who gives piano lessons...Coming back from the inn, Manu was driving pretty wildly. He didn't seem to see the man standing in the road, though everyone else did...there was a bump.

"They stopped and got out. Walking back they found a man lying in the road... *Oui*, Monsieur le Procureur, Mademoiselle Nicole was with them...

"The man was hurt, but very much alive, sufficiently so to tell them he'd have the law on them and make them pay for it. They didn't know what to do. It was Mademoiselle Nicole who kept her head and suggested bringing the man here.

"Yes, without asking him...Monsieur Loursat was told nothing about it.

"The cook?...Yes, she was let into the secret the next day ...I'll be questioning her presently...It was Edmond Dossin who brought Dr. Matray here...The man was found to have a broken leg and a nasty gash three inches long...

"Yes, he's still here."

"He" was Loursat, who paused in his round to pour himself another glass of burgundy.

"I'm sorry, I didn't get that...there's rather a noise going on here...Yes, I asked her whether they'd met since the accident. It seems they've gathered once or twice since then, but not the same as before...She says the injured man was a troublesome creature, always making demands on her..."

Loursat smiled. He appeared to be tickled to learn that a stranger, picked up on the road, had been living in his house for the last two weeks without his knowing it, to say nothing of the doctor's visits (he had been at school with Matray) and the nocturnal revelries of the young people, one of whom, Edmond Dossin, was his nephew, the son of that plaintive, languishing sister of his, whom he couldn't stand and whom he referred to as a pain in the ass.

"Yes, Monsieur le Procureur, I made a particular point of that. And I must say she seemed to be answering me with perfect frankness. She admits Emile Manu came to see her yesterday evening. That's the young man whose mother gives piano lessons. Incidentally she gives them to Mademoiselle Nicole too...Hello?...Hello?...They've cut us off!...Are you there Monsieur le Procureur?...Ah! That's better!...Did you hear what I said?...Well, she and Manu went up to see the invalid, after which they went down to her room..."

An embarrassed look at Loursat, who took that, too, with the utmost calmness. Far from being annoyed, he looked positively jubilant.

"Naturally...It came as a great surprise to me...Yes, there's that possibility. It's quite conceivable. I've had one case myself of a young lady confessing to things she'd certainly never done...But—I may be wrong, of course—but she definitely gave me the impression she was telling the truth...One thing she stated most positively: her visitor left her at about twenty to twelve. She didn't see him out..."

Rogissart, at the other end of the line, made a remark which even amused the humorless Ducup.

"Yes, indeed," he went on, "people seem to walk in and out of the house as if it was a railway station. Apparently the back door, which gives on to l'impasse des Tanneurs, is never locked ...She says it was a few moments after Manu had left her that she heard the shot...She hesitated, wondering what it was and what she ought to do. Before she'd made up her mind, her father had come on the scene...Yes, there are a lot of things to check up...Very good, Monsieur le Procureur. I'll tell him..."

Ducup replaced the receiver and turned toward Loursat with the air of a man who has, at least to some extent, got his own back.

"The prosecutor has asked me to tell you that he's very distressed by the whole affair. He'll do his utmost to keep Mademoiselle Nicole's name out of the papers... You heard what I told him, and I don't think there's anything for me to add. I share the prosecutor's view of the case. It's a very delicate one, a painful one I may say, painful for us all."

"I'd be much obliged if you'd give me the names and addresses of the people on that list of yours."

"I haven't got the full names in every case, nor all the addresses. This is all your daughter was able to give me... I have now to ask you on behalf of the public prosecutor to submit to an official interrogation. After all, it was in your house that the—"

Loursat had already opened the door and was shouting into the corridor: "Send up the magistrate's clerk."

Getting no response, he walked toward the stairs.

"Hello, there!... Can't anybody hear me?... Send up the magistrate's clerk..."

Rogissart was no doubt at that moment telephoning to Mme Dossin and the latter was no doubt reclining on a sofa draped in muslins that were probably mauve. She'd be looking distinguished of course. Looking distinguished and being in delicate health combined to provide her with a full-time occupation, leaving her perhaps just sufficient energy to arrange a few flowers in a vase.

She was as unlike her brother as it was possible to be. She was the refined one of the family. She had married Dossin, who in a more robust way made much the same pretensions to elegance as she did. In the quarter that lay behind the promenade they had built themselves the most luxurious house in Moulins, and it was one of the very few where a white-gloved butler waited at table.

Loursat grinned. He could almost hear his cousin say, "Hello! ... My dear friend, such a dreadful thing has happened... But first of all, how are you?... Oh, dear!... I'm so sorry... and I'm afraid what I have to tell you will come as a blow to you... The thing is, your son... Yes, of course, we're doing all we can to..."

And having first rung for her maid, Mme Dossin would no doubt pass off into a comfortable faint amongst her cushions and her flowers.

"Did you call me, Monsieur le Juge?"

"Yes. I want you to take down Monsieur Loursat's statement."

"Hector Dominique François Loursat de Saint-Marc," recited the lawyer in his most caustic voice. "Lawyer. Member of the Moulins Bar... Age forty-eight... Husband of Geneviève Loursat, née Grosillière, now of unknown address."

The clerk looked up, wondering whether he ought to write down the last words.

"Go on, write," said Loursat. "Except that she has been taking her meals with me as usual, I know nothing of the actions of my daughter, Nicole Loursat. I know nothing of what has been going on in this house other than in my personal quarters, which consist of this study and the bedroom adjoining. I might add that I regard what goes on in other parts of the house as no concern of mine...

"Last night, that is to say the night of Wednesday to Thursday, having heard an unusual noise, which sounded like a revolver shot, I made the mistake of concerning myself with the matter. On going to a room on the third floor, I discovered a man lying in bed, who died a few seconds later of a gunshot wound. I have nothing further to say."

He turned to Ducup who had been fidgeting in his chair. "A cigarette?"

"No thank you."

"A glass of burgundy?"

"I think I told you—"

"Of course! You never drink at this time of day. Oh, well! That's your misfortune! And now..."

He broke off and waited, making it quite clear that he considered his interrogation at an end and wished to be left alone.

"If you'll excuse me," said Ducup, making the best of his dismissal, "I'll now put a few questions to your cook. As for the maid who left your service last night, we're looking for her now. You'll understand better than anybody."

"Better than anybody, yes!"

"Inspector Binet has sent a photograph of the dead man to Paris together with his fingerprints."

It was for no particular reason that Loursat muttered, "Poor Binet!"

"He's a most conscientious officer, I assure you."

"Yes, yes. Most conscientious."

He hadn't yet got to the end of the first bottle. He'd drunk enough, however, to dispel the morning's ill humor, the bad taste in his mouth, and the fuzzy feeling in his head.

"It's possible that I may have to—"

"Anything you like—"

"But—"

But Loursat had had enough. He opened the door.

"You must admit I've done all I could to—"

"Yes, Monsieur Ducup."

And even that simple "Monsieur Ducup" could be pronounced in such a way as to turn it into a term of contempt.

"As for the newspapermen—"

"You'll deal effectively with them, I'm sure."

And the sooner the magistrate was out of that room the better for him and everybody else. It was hard to think in peace with Ducup's ugly mug in front of him.

He shook hands abruptly with both of them and bundled them into the passage.

Locking the door behind them, he heaved a sigh of relief, then frowned as he realized that Ducup had left behind him an objectionable smell of hair lotion.

So Nicole had been...

He poked the fire vigorously, causing the flames to flare up and almost singe his legs.

Nicole...

Twice he walked around his room, filled his glass right up to the brim, and drank it, standing, at a single swallow. Then he sat down and studied the sheet of paper on which he had written down the young people's names.

Nicole...

He had taken her for a gawky, overgrown schoolgirl. And now...

A car drove off, probably with Ducup. The house was fairly swarming with people.

But Nicole?...What would she be doing now?

3

HE DIDN'T laugh. He barely even smiled. It was more a sensation of surprise, followed immediately by a feeling of joy and jubilation, washing over him like a hot bath.

It was almost one o'clock. Loursat had strolled into the dining room, where he had found Phine laying the table, her movements, like the look on her face, betraying her irritation.

For no particular reason, he decided to remain there, and he stood with his back to the miserable smoking fire, watching her as she worked. After three or four impatient movements, Phine snatched up the knives and forks from the sideboard drawer and banged them down on the table, and when that failed to have an effect she snarled, "I didn't ring, did I?"

He looked at her with some surprise. He was astonished to realize how small she was, how ugly and disagreeable. He wasn't far from wondering how she came to be there. At the same time he noticed that the drawer from which she had taken the knives and forks had in his day been used for the tablecloth and napkins. It struck him forcibly how completely he had withdrawn himself not to have noticed such a change before.

On other days he waited for the bell to ring before emerging from his lair, and even when it did ring he rarely responded at once. Sometimes a quarter of an hour would elapse before he'd finally make up his mind to move, and, when he reached the dining room, he'd find Nicole reading a book to fill in the time.

When he appeared, the girl would put down the book without a word and give the maid a look which was the signal for her to start serving the meal.

And now for the first time it was he who had got there first. For a moment he was at a loss to understand why Phine should have come up from the depths of her kitchen to set the table. Then he remembered that the housemaid had left the previous evening.

It was all very odd. He would not have been capable, had he been questioned, of saying just what was odd or why. It was odd, all the same. He had a vague impression of newness in his surroundings. There he was in his own house, in the house where he had been born and in which he had lived ever since. And all of a sudden it struck him as extraordinary that a huge bell should be rung, as in a monastery, to summon two persons to a meal.

Phine left the room without another glance at him. She hated him with all the venom of which she was capable, and she made no bones about it. To Nicole she would say, "That dirty old father of yours..."

The bell rang and a few moments later Nicole appeared, looking calm, almost serene. No one could have guessed that this girl of twenty had just been through an official interrogation of nearly two hours.

She hadn't shed a tear, and now, as she came into the room, she seemed to have banished the subject from her mind. She glanced at the table to see that everything was in its place, just like any other mistress of the house, then went over to the dumbwaiter, opened the hatch, and gently called down into the shaft:

"We're all ready, Phine."

Like any mistress of the house! The idea suddenly struck Loursat. That's what Nicole was: the mistress of the house. He had never seen her in that light before. And now, since there was no maid to wait, she did the job herself, carrying the dishes to the table before taking her place.

Without a word. Without a single glance at her father.

Without the slightest sign of curiosity about his reactions to what had happened!

He did his best to play his part as usual. He ate and drank loudly and spilled more than ever onto his waistcoat. But it was no use. He couldn't prevent his thoughts from constantly reverting to Nicole. On other days he had been able to gaze in her direction almost without seeing her. Now he kept *wanting to look at her*. He was shy of doing so openly and merely stole furtive glances at her from time to time.

Still more extraordinary, he would even have liked to talk to her, to exchange a few casual words with her, no matter what about, just for the sake of hearing her voice instead of the eternal scrape of knives and forks and the occasional splutter of a briquette in the grate.

"Phine! The next course, please!" she called down the shaft.

If she was on the plump side, she was not in the least flabby. Indeed it was the suggestion of firmness in her which surprised Loursat more than anything. Her placidness was not inertia. In it was a quiet latent strength.

In spite of himself he fished in his pocket and pulled out a crumpled bit of paper. As he opened it, shreds of tobacco fell from it onto his plate. On it were the names Ducup had given him that morning.

"What does he do, this Emile Manu?"

He felt awkward at having broken a silence that had lasted so many years. It almost made him blush. It wasn't merely a tradition that he was betraying; it was his own personality.

At first, she turned her big eyes on him in wonderment, then she looked at the bit of paper and understood.

"He works in a bookshop, the Librairie Georges."

For a second it looked as though they were going to have a real conversation. If she had enlarged on the subject even a little, they probably would have.

But she merely answered his question and left it at that. To cover his embarrassment, he stared hard at the paper, chewing more loudly than ever.

He was in the habit of taking a short walk at three o'clock every afternoon. It was the sort of walk you take to exercise a small dog, in fact he almost gave the impression of holding himself on a leash. The walk consisted of going around four blocks of houses, never more, never less.

This time he hadn't taken two steps before he once again broke with tradition. He stopped. He turned. He stood on the curb contemplating his house.

It was impossible to tell what was going on in his mind or whether his train of thought was pleasant or unpleasant. Only one thing was quite definite: it was extraordinary! He saw his house. He saw it as he had seen it as a child, or as a young man when he came back for his holidays from Paris where he was studying law.

Not that the sight touched him. That would never have done. He couldn't possibly have allowed it. He was a surly, intractable man.

All the same, it was curious to think that... Well, those evenings... when those young people gathered up there on the third floor... They'd have to put some lights on, wouldn't they? And those lights would glimmer through the slats of the shutters making the house seem...

And that back door that was never locked... Would the neighbors have noticed people sneaking in and out?

And Nicole in her bedroom with that... that...

He had to consult his list. Manu! Emile Manu! Didn't that fit in quite well with the figure he'd caught sight of on the stairs? A young man in a beige overcoat.

And when those two were shut up together in her room, did they...?

He slouched off, nodding his head, his hands clasped behind his round back, and suddenly he came to a halt in front of a little girl who was staring at him. She must be one of the neighbors' children. There was a time when he had known who lived in every house on the street. But that was long ago. Since then some people had moved, others had died. Inevitably some had been born!

This little girl would be one of them. Why was she so interested in him? Why was she afraid of him?

Perhaps her parents had told her he was a wicked man, or even an ogre!

A little further on, he was surprised to find himself muttering, "So she takes piano lessons, does she?"

His mind had worked back to Nicole. Now and again he had heard a piano being played in the house. An unpleasant sound it was too! It fitted in with his idea of Nicole as an overgrown schoolgirl. Didn't all girls learn the piano at school? He supposed so.

But he had never dreamed she *studied music.* He didn't even know she liked it . . . How had she come to choose that particular teacher? Probably Mme Manu was that gray-haired woman he occasionally passed on the stairs and who bowed to him ceremoniously . . .

It was all very strange! Still stranger that he had now reached the rue d'Allier, which was off his usual route. He only realized it when he found himself staring at the Librairie Georges, a dismal old-fashioned shop, so dark inside that at first sight you'd have thought it closed.

He walked in and recognized the old man, Georges, who had already seemed old when Loursat was a boy. He was grumpy and full of ill will. He wore a forage cap and his forbidding appearance was completed by a walrus moustache and bushy eyebrows like Clemenceau's.

He was standing at a high desk writing, and he didn't even

look up to see who had entered his shop. In the back, lit up by an inadequate electric lamp, were the rows and rows of buckram-bound books of the lending library. A young man promptly climbed down from the ladder that stood in front of the shelves.

At first he stepped forward quite naturally. An ordinary young man such as one could find in pretty well any bookshop or for that matter in any other sort of shop. He had not yet finished growing. A long, scraggy neck, rather fair hair, features that lacked firmness.

Suddenly he stopped. He must have recognized the lawyer. Perhaps someone had pointed him out in the street. Perhaps he'd even seen him at home, since he was one of the many people who had the run of the house!

He turned pale and stood there, braced taut from head to foot, glancing this way and that as though looking for a possible way of escape.

And Loursat was surprised to find himself looking at the boy fiercely.

"What do you—What can I—"

He couldn't finish his sentence. His throat was tight. His Adam's apple went up and down above his pale blue tie.

The old bookseller raised his head, wondering what was amiss.

"Give me a book, young man," growled the lawyer.

"What book, Monsieur?"

"Any one you like."

"Show Monsieur the latest publications," interposed the bookseller.

The boy darted off, almost knocking over a pile of books. He really was a boy. Not yet nineteen. Perhaps only seventeen. Thin as an overgrown chick. No, not a chick, a young cockerel that is just beginning to take itself seriously.

And this was the fellow who had driven the car that night...

Loursat snorted. He was annoyed with himself for thinking

about it. Why should he take an interest in this subject? For eighteen years he had stood firm, and now, just because of some silly tomfoolery...

"That'll do. I'll take it...No, you needn't wrap it up."

He spoke curtly, harshly.

"How much is it?"

"Eighteen francs, Monsieur. I'll give you a jacket."

"I can do without."

He walked out of the shop, stuffing the book into his pocket. He felt he needed a drink. He hardly recognized the rue d'Allier, though it was the main street of Moulins. For instance, beside a gunsmith's that had always been there, he found a fixed-price bazaar, Prisunic, with goods set out on stalls on the sidewalk, piles of cheeses jostling woolens on one side, and popular songs on the other. Overhead hung big white balls that would soon be shedding a glaring light on these heterogeneous wares.

A little further down the street he came to a pork butcher's. Three large windows in a marble frontage. Looking up, he read: Charcuterie Daillat.

Daillat! That was another of the names on his list. Another who frequented his house at strange hours.

Would he be serving in the shop? Loursat looked in to see. A number of girls in white, looking very fresh and pink, were rushing to and fro at an incredible speed. There was one man in a striped suit and a white apron...No! It couldn't be him. He had a florid face with practically no neck at all and couldn't be a day under forty...Ah! There was another! A young ginger-haired man dressed just the same, who was busy slicing cutlets...

Undoubtedly a very prosperous business. To think that a little town like Moulins could eat so much!

What was the bar they'd said the young people went to? He hadn't taken down the name, but he remembered it was near the marketplace, which lay in a dismal quarter with narrow streets.

He turned down one of them. The Boxing Bar. That was it: he could remember now. A small front, with lattice windows and check curtains designed to give a rustic effect. Inside, the room was small, furnished only with two fumed-oak tables and chairs and a little bar with high stools.

It was empty. Loursat rolled up to the bar like a bear, bad tempered and mistrustful, looking disapprovingly first at the photos of actors and boxers stuck on the mirrors, then at the high stools and the paraphernalia of cocktails.

A man bobbed up behind the counter like a jack-in-the-box, since he had to dive through a hole in the side of it to get there.

He wore a white jacket and was chewing something. He looked at the lawyer and frowned. Picking up a napkin, he muttered, "What do you want?"

Did he too know Loursat? . . . Did he too know what had happened? . . . It certainly looked like it.

He was an unprepossessing fellow. With his receding forehead and broken nose it wasn't hard to guess he'd been a boxer or a wrestler.

"Have you got any red wine?"

Still chewing, the other held a bottle up to the light to see if there was anything in it, then, with a bored expression on his face, poured out a glass. The wine was corked. Loursat made no comments, however, and asked no questions. Leaving the place, he quickened his pace, hurried away from the dreary district, and reached home in a bad humor.

He must have gone up the stairs, since he had reached the second floor, but he hadn't been conscious of doing so. He switched on the passage light and made for his study. He felt something hard bulging in his overcoat pocket, realized it was the book he'd bought, and growled, "Fool!"

He was longing to get back into his own den and slam the padded door that shut out the world. He was longing to—

On the threshold he suddenly stopped, frowned, and snapped at someone inside: "What are you doing there?"

Poor Inspector Binet! He hadn't expected such a welcome. He hastily jumped to his feet and began pouring out his profuse and ever-ready apologies. Joséphine had shown him into the room when it was still daylight. She had abandoned him to his fate, and the inspector had gone on sitting demurely with his hat on his knees in the gathering twilight, and finally in total darkness.

"I thought I ought to keep you informed . . . considering that the crime was committed in your house."

Like a man recovering his belongings, Loursat threw a possessive glance at his stove, his burgundy, his cigarettes, and even sniffed the study's familiar smell to make sure that it too had not been tampered with.

"Very well! What have you found out? . . . Will you have a glass of wine?"

"With pleasure."

Loursat had merely offered it as an unavoidable politeness and the inspector's acceptance came as a surprise. The latter realized he'd made a mistake when the lawyer was unable to find a second glass in the cupboard, and he made haste to undo the mischief by protesting, "Please don't bother. It's all the same to me."

But Loursat wouldn't listen to him. The man had accepted a glass of wine, hadn't he? Very well! He was going to have one! Even though it did mean getting a glass from the dining room.

It wasn't easy to find one, but eventually the lawyer returned and with an almost fierce determination filled it to the brim.

"There you are! . . . Now what were you saying?"

"That I wanted to keep you informed. Besides, you may be

able to help us. I've already heard from Paris. They called me a little while ago. They've identified the dead man. He was an undesirable, in fact quite a dangerous individual called Louis Gagalin, better known by his nickname, Big Louie. I'll let you have a copy of the particulars they gave me. Briefly, he was born in a village in the Cantal. At seventeen, when working as a farm laborer, he assaulted his employer, who had accused him of being drunk; he struck him several times with a spade and very nearly killed him. For that he was put in a reformatory, where he remained four years and where he was regarded as a thoroughly bad character. He was released two years ago and since then has been constantly in trouble with the police."

Another of Loursat's guests! He had stayed for two weeks! Only, of course, his host hadn't been aware of it!

"I haven't seen any of the young people concerned. Monsieur Ducup wants to question them himself, one by one. But I've had a talk with Dr. Matray, who made no bones about telling me all he knew. That is, one evening, or rather night, as it was one o'clock in the morning, he was brought here by Edmond Dossin, who appealed to him to observe the strictest secrecy. Upstairs he found Big Louie suffering from pretty serious injuries caused by the car that the group had taken for their escapade. He set the broken leg and bandaged him up. Three times he called in again to see him, and each time it was Mademoiselle Nicole who received him. On two occasions Emile Manu was present."

Loursat had by this time recovered his normal bearing. He seemed bored, aloof, contemptuous.

"To come to the more serious part of the case, there seems to be no doubt whatever that Big Louie was killed by a shot fired at point-blank range from a 6.35-millimeter revolver. We've found the cartridge case, but so far no trace of the weapon."

"He took it away with him," stated Loursat as though he had personal knowledge of the fact.

"Yes. Or hid it somewhere. Anyhow it's a pity we can't find it. It would help a lot."

The inspector got up.

"I don't think there's any more for us to do here," he said. "But if you'd like me to keep you informed..."

He had been gone a good five minutes when Loursat muttered under his breath, "What an odd little man!"

Then: "Whatever did he want to come and see me for? He certainly hadn't much to tell me!"

He looked at his desk, at the stove, at the half-empty bottle, at the easy chair in which Inspector Binet had been sitting, then, as though painfully dragging himself from them, he got up with a sigh, opened the door, and wandered off to explore for himself.

He had scarcely reached the main staircase when someone jumped up in front of him, someone who had apparently been sitting there waiting for a considerable time, just as the inspector had in the study.

It took him a moment to recognize Angèle, the maid who'd left the previous day, but that was partly because he'd never before seen her street clothes. She wore a navy-blue tailored dress with a cream silk blouse that exaggerated her already very ample bust. Her little hat was quite neat and sober, but beneath it her face was horribly made up, her cheeks plastered with a purplish rouge and her eyelids penciled with blue.

"Tell me! Is she going to make up her mind to see me or isn't she?"

It was quite unexpected. Loursat was somewhat bewildered. What really staggered him was the blatant vulgarity of the girl, a vulgarity he could never have suspected as she moved silently between the dumbwaiter and the dining-room table, carrying dishes.

"How much are you going to give me?"

Then, as he apparently didn't understand her: "I suppose

you're drunk again! No. It's too early in the day for that. Perhaps you don't want to understand! But it's no use. You can't frighten me with those big eyes of yours any more than your daughter can with all her airs and graces. I've got an account to settle with her, and I'm not going till it is settled. I go home for a holiday and I've hardly had time to say how do you do to my parents when what happens? The gendarmes come and drag me off without a word of explanation. As though I was a common thief!... Then at the Palais de Justice they keep me waiting a whole hour, so that I get no dinner at all—and all because of that bitch of a daughter of yours and her goings on at all hours of the night..."

He was less interested in the words than in their tone and the hatred it betrayed, and he was still lost in wonderment at the contrast presented by this creature standing in front of him and the girl he remembered in a black dress and white apron.

"I guess you don't know what village folk are like. Do you think they'll believe the gendarmes came to get me for nothing? If they start asking around there'll be people ready to put in a bad word about me. And that's what you've got to pay for. You're rich enough, even if you do live like pigs."

Live like pigs... the words hit home. With a puzzled look on his face he looked around at the dilapidated house.

"Come on! What'll you give me?"

"What did you say to the examining magistrate?"

"Everything! I told him just what went on here—things that no reasonable person would have believed, that is, not if *this* hadn't happened. I thought when I came here you were both a little crazy. Or all three of you—that old witch downstairs is no better. She's the meanest old hag I've ever met, but that's neither here nor there. What I'm talking about is the wild parties that went on up at the top of the house when decent people ought to be in bed."

Perhaps it would have been better to shut her up. Yet why

should he? It was curious. He found himself listening to her with something like genuine interest, though the most interesting thing to his mind was why she should take it all so much to heart.

"By the look of her you'd think butter wouldn't melt in her mouth, and by the way she was always getting onto me, hauling me over the coals for this and that, you'd have said she could never have put up for a moment with anything that wasn't quite right, yet she wasn't above raiding your wine cellar behind your back and dancing and playing the phonograph till four in the morning. As for drinking, she could put it away like any man."

Ah! So there was a phonograph in the house! And they used to dance!

"You should have seen the mess I had to clear up in the mornings. I thought myself lucky when they hadn't been sick all over the place. Sometimes I'd find one of them in bed—one who'd been too drunk to carry himself home. A pretty state of affairs! And, with that, you treat your servants as though—"

Loursat looked up. He had heard a slight noise, and now, looking past Angèle along the ill-lit passage, he saw his daughter, who had just come out of her room. She was standing still, listening.

He didn't say anything and the next moment Angèle had started off again.

"So perhaps you've got an idea by now what I told the examining magistrate. Indeed in the end he was doing his best to stop me! I told him that the best place for the lot of them was prison, and your daughter too . . . Only of course there are some people who never get put in prison! But if you want to find out the truth, ask her what there was in the parcels. Still better, ask her for the key to the loft, and if you do I don't mind betting nobody'll be able to find it. And that poor sap, the one that was killed, he wasn't any better.

"Well, have you heard enough? There's no use staring at me like that, you know. I reckon the harm you've done me and the time it's wasted is worth a thousand francs."

Nicole was still there and he wondered whether she was going to intervene.

"Did you tell the examining magistrate you were coming here to demand money?"

"I told him I was going to claim damages. And it wasn't hard to see what was going on in his mind and that his one idea was to hush everything up as much as possible. Of course he didn't say so plainly. He beat about the bush for half an hour to tell me that the inquiry was only just starting and that for the moment the least said about it the better... blah, blah... Why? Because the people concerned are moneyed people! And it's not hard to see what'll happen. They'll go on inquiring and inquiring till everybody's forgotten about it and then quietly drop it. Never mind about the guy that was killed. He doesn't count."

"I'll give you a thousand francs."

Not because he was afraid. Not to make her keep her mouth shut. But because in some obscure way he felt she'd earned it!

He toddled back to his study to get the money, taking the opportunity of having another glass of burgundy. When he returned Angèle was sitting quietly, musing over her unexpected victory.

"Thanks!" she said folding the notes and putting them in her bag.

Was her conscience pricking her? She looked at Loursat out of the corner of her eye.

"Don't think I've anything against you personally. The thing is—"

She broke off. Probably the thought was too vague to be put into words. Besides, she'd got her money, hadn't she? What was the point of talking now? But she wasn't entirely reassured.

"Don't disturb yourself. I'll close the door behind me."

He was left standing face to face with his daughter, who was only a few yards away, wearing a light-colored dress.

She didn't turn back into her room at once. Presumably she thought he was going to speak to her.

He wanted to. He was about to open his mouth.

But what was he to say to her?

Everything he thought of sounded somehow false. The truth was, he felt shy of opening up. And she understood so well that she turned away without a word and went back to her room.

Where had he been going when he'd bumped into Angèle? He tried to remember, but without much success. The truth was that he hadn't had any precise destination in view, he'd set out to explore. No doubt that meant going upstairs, but that was all.

What had Angèle meant when she'd spoken of the loft? And which loft had she been referring to? There were three separate ones in the house. And the parcels? Parcels of what?

He realized that his telephone had been ringing for at least a minute. As usual, his reaction had been to ignore it as long as possible, until in fact it got on his nerves.

Once more he was back in his study and the warm stagnation that belonged to it, and to him. Why did he ever leave it?

"Hello? ... Who is it? ... Oh, Marthe ... What do you want?"

His sister. It was a wonder she hadn't rung up sooner. He could picture her reclining on a sofa with the receiver in her hand.

"I warn you that if you're going to cry I won't be able to hear what you say."

It was a mystery to everybody how this tall, pale, drooping flower of a woman came to be his sister.

"Serves him right! Do him good!"

He sat down and filled up his glass again. Marthe had just been telling him that her son, Edmond, had been summoned to the Palais de Justice.

"What on earth are you talking about? ... Me?"

It was priceless! His sister was blaming him for being the cause of all the trouble, by having brought Nicole up so badly.

"You want me to intervene on his behalf. I'll do nothing of the sort ... Prison, you say? ... Well, what's wrong with prison? ... Knock some of the nonsense out of him ... Now, look here, Marthe! Listen! You're a pain in the ass ... Yes, you heard right. Goodbye ..."

It had been a long time since such a thing had happened to him and he was quite troubled about it. He had actually become angry. He had got hot all over. He was fairly tingling with it.

"Ah, but—" Breathing heavily, he picked up his glass then put it down again. He reflected. Perhaps he didn't want to dope himself into a semi-stupor as he did every other day.

The shutters were still open and the windows were a dark satiny blue spotted with lights. Now and then people hurried past.

He suddenly thought of the rue d'Allier. He didn't care to ask himself whether he wanted to be back there in the crowd in the glaring lights of the Prisunic or in front of that busy pork butcher's shop.

At that time would the Librairie Georges be shutting? Perhaps at that very moment Emile Manu was putting on his grubby beige mackintosh. What would he do? Where would he go?

He ought to have spoken to Nicole ...

Anyhow she seemed to be taking it pretty calmly. As for all the others, they must be scared stiff: the butcher's son, the bank clerk, and that young fool, the Dossin boy who had to be taken off to the mountains every year, as he was supposed to be delicate, like his mother, while his father took the opportunity of going off somewhere or other "on business," which really meant having a grand time with the girls!

The people who were most upset of all would undoubtedly

be the Rogissarts. During the whole of his career, the public prosecutor had been afraid of trouble.

Now he'd got one! Right between the eyes! And no doubt he'd spend half the night discussing with his wife how to minimize the damage.

As he mused, Loursat fished the crumpled bit of paper out of his pocket and spread it out before him on his desk.

Dossin . . . Daillat . . . Destrivaux . . . Manu . . .

And that other, the dead man who went by the name of Big Louie. What was his real name? Oh yes, Louis Gagalan.

In his heavy hand Loursat added that name to the others. Having done so, he came to the conclusion it would have been more suitable to use red ink!

He drank the wine after all. It was probably better that way. There was safety in habit. He carefully poked the fire, stoked it up, and regulated the draft. No reason to change one's habits just because of . . .

Because of what? That was the question.

The door opened though no one had knocked. It was Phine, ungracious as ever. "There's a young man downstairs who wants to see you."

"Who is it?"

"He didn't give any name. I know all the same."

She made him ask, however, "Who is it then?"

"Monsieur Emile."

And the old hag pronounced the name as if it was the sweetest sound in the world. Obviously the boy was a pet of hers and she was ready to stand up for him against all the world.

"I suppose you mean Emile Manu."

"Monsieur Emile," she corrected. "Will you see him or won't you?"

Emile meanwhile was all alone, pacing feverishly up and down the huge paved hall, peering every minute up the dimly lit stairs at the top of which Joséphine eventually appeared.

"You can come up," she said.

And Loursat, to fortify himself for the interview, quickly poured himself another glass and swallowed it almost furtively.

4

"SIT DOWN."

But Emile was too highly strung to be able to go through the usual formalities of a visit. He'd hardly had time to sense the atmosphere in the hot, stuffy room before he burst out, "I've come to tell you—"

Loursat had no intention of being aggressive, but perhaps he was inwardly up in arms against something. Anyhow he suddenly shouted at the top of his voice: "For God's sake, will you sit down!"

Admittedly he always hated to be sitting while the person he was talking to stood. That, however, was no reason to let fly. For his part, the young man was so disconcerted that he hadn't even the presence of mind to look around him for a chair. He was wearing his grubby beige mackintosh and his suit, to judge from what was visible, was of the sort you see hanging up outside shops of ready-made clothes. His shoes were cracked and down at heel, and no doubt had been resoled many times.

In the end Loursat jumped to his feet, drew a chair forward, and pushed Emile into it. Then, satisfied at last, he sat down again with a sigh of relief.

"You'd come to tell me what?"

The young man couldn't answer. The lawyer's sudden outburst had cut the ground from under his feet. All the same, it was with anything but a hang-dog air that he looked at him.

Indeed his expression was a strange mixture of humility and pride.

For instance, in the very way in which he looked straight into Loursat's eye, he seemed to be saying, "Don't get the idea I'm afraid of you!"

It was excessive nervous tension, not fear, that made his lips quiver and his fingers clutch convulsively at the hat he was holding.

"I know what you're thinking," he said at last, "and why you came to the shop this afternoon."

Though there was a slight tremor in his voice, it was now he who was on the offensive. His words plainly signified: "You may be a great lawyer and all that, but I can see what's going on in your mind."

Loursat wondered whether he himself had been like Emile at that age, thin and bony, jerky in his movements, with eyes that watched people jealously and were quick to take offense. How would he at the age of eighteen have stood up to a man of forty-eight?

Emile Manu's voice was firmer when he came out with: "It wasn't me that killed Big Louie."

Still tense, he waited for his opponent to retort.

"How did you know Big Louie was killed?" asked the lawyer, a faint smile spreading over his face.

Instantly Emile saw his mistake. He oughtn't to have known of the crime since the one and only local paper hadn't so much as mentioned it. Even the neighbors, though they might have caught a glimpse of the body being carried out of the house on a stretcher, would have had no means of knowing it was the body of a man who had been killed.

"I just know."

"Then somebody must have told you."

"Yes. I got a note from Nicole this afternoon!"

He looked straight at Loursat. "You see, I have nothing to hide," he seemed to be saying. "You can stare at me as hard as you like and watch my reactions, you won't find anything; there's nothing there to find."

As though to prove it, he took the note from his pocket. "Here it is. You can read it."

It was undoubtedly Nicole's tall, neat writing.

Big Louie is dead. The examining magistrate had me on the rack for two whole hours. I told him everything about our meetings—the car accident included—and gave him the names of those who took part.

That was all. There was no "Dear Emile" at the beginning, no signature at the end.

"Had you already received this note when I called at the bookshop this afternoon?"

"Yes."

"Who brought it to you?"

"Phine. She had several notes, in fact one for each of us."

So as soon as Ducup had done with her, Nicole had quickly written half a dozen notes to the others. And Phine had trotted all around the town to deliver them.

"There's one thing I don't understand, young man. Why do you come to me to tell me you didn't kill Big Louie?"

"Because you saw me!"

This time he was frankly defiant.

"I knew you'd seen me and would recognize me sooner or later. In fact that's why you came to the shop. If you tell the police, I'll be arrested right away."

The strange mixture of elements within him was never more evident. He spoke the words with the firmness of a man, yet the next moment his lower lip was drawn up like that of a child about to burst into tears, and his features seemed to dissolve, becoming so irresolute as to make one wonder how one had been able to take him seriously.

"If they arrest me, my mother…"

But no! He wasn't going to break down! He clenched his fists and sprang to his feet. There was hatred in his eyes, hatred for this man who could so humiliate him while calmly sipping his wine.

"I can see you don't believe me. In that case I shall be locked up and my mother will lose all her pupils."

"Gently! Gently! Will you have a glass of wine? No?…Just as you like…I notice you speak of your mother, not of your father."

"He died long ago."

"What did he do?"

"He was a draftsman. He worked at Dossin's."

"Do you live alone with your mother?"

"Yes. I'm her only child."

"Where?"

"Rue Ernest-Voivenon."

A new street on the outskirts, not far from the cemetery. Humble houses for humble folk. That Emile hated living there was obvious from the challenging way he threw out the name, following it up with, "What does it matter to you where I live?"

"I've already asked you to sit down."

"Excuse me."

"Since you admit to being the person I saw on the back stairs, perhaps you'll tell me what you were doing up on the top floor. You had just left Nicole's room, presumably to go straight home."

"Yes."

What would he, Hector Loursat, have felt like had he at eighteen or nineteen found himself in Emile's shoes? The boy was sitting before a father whose daughter's room he had left at close to midnight!

Oddly enough, now that they had reached the most controversial issue, Emile was much calmer.

"I was making my way to the back door. I had just reached the stairs when I heard the shot. Instead of hurrying away, I went up—I don't know why. Someone came out of Big Louie's room—"

"You saw who it was?"

"No. There was no light on."

Again he looked squarely at Loursat, as though determined to convince him of his truthfulness.

"Go on."

"The man must have heard me."

"So it was a man?"

"I was merely assuming it was."

"It couldn't have been Nicole?"

"Impossible. I'd only turned my back on her a few seconds when the shot was fired."

"Where had you left her?"

"At the door of her room."

"What did the man do?"

"He ran away down the passage and slipped through a door and shut it. Having gone so far, I suppose I should have followed. I was afraid, and came downstairs—"

"Without stopping to see what had become of Big Louie?"

"Yes."

"Did you leave the house at once?"

"No. I stood by the back door listening while you and Nicole went up."

"So there was another fellow in the house besides you?"

"I swear there was."

Then, becoming more voluble, "I came to ask you, if it's not already too late, to say nothing of having seen me. My mother's had trouble enough in her life. I don't want this to fall back on her... We only have just enough, as it is, to make both ends meet."

Loursat sat motionless, and the reading lamp on the desk

left him more or less in the shadow, where he looked heavier and bulkier than ever.

"There's another thing I wanted to say to you."

The boy's spirit had sagged again on mentioning his mother. Now once more he looked up sharply, challengingly.

"I wanted to ask your permission to marry Nicole. If this dreadful thing hadn't happened, I'd have waited till . . ."

Till he was earning a decent livelihood, of course. He couldn't keep away from this question of money, which haunted him, which hemmed him in on every side. The more he struggled against it, the more conscious he was of his inferiority, and that in turn made him aggressive.

"You're thinking of leaving the bookshop?"

"You don't expect me to stay in a job like that all my life, do you?"

"No. Of course not. You were thinking of going to Paris, perhaps . . ."

"Yes."

"To make your fortune."

Emile picked up the note of sarcasm.

"I don't know whether I'd have made a fortune, but I don't see why I shouldn't have got on as well as other people do."

There! He was crying at last, the little fool! No. That was unfair. It was really Loursat's fault for not knowing how to handle him.

"I love Nicole. And she loves me."

"I have every reason to think so, since she receives you in her room at night!"

There he was! Being sarcastic again! Why couldn't he be gentler? Just because he couldn't! He fully realized that to a boy like this Emile he must seem a terrible man.

"We've sworn we'd get married."

Having rummaged in all his pockets, Emile at last found a handkerchief and was able to wipe his eyes and blow his nose.

"How long have you known Nicole?"

It was a moment before Emile answered. "For quite a long time. She used often to come to the shop to borrow books from the library."

"That's how you became friends, is it?"

"Not exactly. In the shop I was only a..."

Up it cropped again. Always this question of the mediocrity of his situation.

"And then my mother talked about her. She's been coming here for some time. It was by giving piano lessons that she was able to keep me on at school after my father died. She came at eleven in the morning, but most of the time she was sent away again, as Nicole was still in bed..."

He was calming down, and it was almost in a chatty tone that he went on.

"It was Luska who introduced me to the group."

"Who's Luska?"

"Don't you know his father's shop? Just opposite the boys' school. They sell toys, candy, marbles, fishing rods, and all sorts of things. The kid works at the toy counter in Prisunic."

Loursat looked away a little sheepishly. The mention of the boys' school and marbles had taken him back thirty-eight years. In those days there was no shop there at all, but only an old woman, *la mère* Pinaud, who kept a little sweet stall where they bought jujubes as they came out of school...

If the young man hadn't been there, Loursat might have got up and looked in the glass to contemplate almost with aston-ishment the changes which the lapse of a generation had wrought in his face.

"So Luska introduced you... Where was that?"

"At Joe's."

"Who's Joe?"

"A retired boxer who runs the Boxing Bar, near the market-place."

What was most troubling was to be living on two different levels at the same moment. On the one hand Loursat was sitting just as usual at his desk, his fat haunches filling up his chair, his dirty fingers with their black-edged nails scratching his head or fidgeting with his beard. He had his bottle on one side, his stove on the other, and rows and rows of books all around the walls.

But at the same time, he was conscious of being there. He could see Hector Loursat sitting there, hear his voice when he spoke, and be aware of his age, his dirty nails, his surliness. It was a thing that had never happened to him before.

"I was a slip of a boy too," he mused. "Just about as thin as he is."

He was much less sociable, however. He'd spent most of his time alone, reading poetry and philosophy and getting excited about ideas. Perhaps that was the source of all the trouble. He tried to see himself as he then was, particularly when he was courting Geneviève.

Emile, meanwhile, little suspecting the other's thoughts, was going on with his story.

"We went off in the car. There was the accident. I've never been lucky. It's in the family. My father died at thirty-two."

Loursat was quite surprised to hear himself asking, "What of?"

"Pneumonia. It started with a cold he caught when he took us to an aviation show. It rained and he got wet through."

Somebody else had died young of pneumonia... Oh, yes! Geneviève's brother. He was still younger. Only twenty-four. He died only a few weeks after their marriage.

He couldn't find any cigarettes on his desk, and this annoyed him. It seemed to him that between Geneviève's day and now was not so much a void as a vast evil-smelling morass.

And he was still floundering in it!

No! No! What was the matter with him? Where on earth was this ridiculous young man leading him?

"You helped yourself to someone else's car, I believe?"

"Edmond told me that's what they always did when Daillat couldn't get the van."

"I see. Normally you went out in the butcher's van?"

"Yes. The garage is a ways from the house, so his father couldn't hear him take it."

"In fact I suppose none of the parents knew anything at all! What did you do at Joe's?"

"Edmond taught me to play écarté and poker."

So, one more person who'd be wearing a funny expression— his sister, Marthe. Edmond's case was most astonishing of all: a big kid, but soft, with pink cheeks and girlish eyes, always hovering over his sick mother.

"Was Edmond the leader?"

"More or less. There wasn't one really, but the others generally fell in with his suggestions."

How much of all this had his mother found out?

"Since I was new, they made me drink. Then Edmond suggested a trip."

"Nicole came with you, of course."

"Yes."

"Did she pair off with anybody in particular?"

Emile reddened.

"As a matter of fact, I thought so too at first. Later she swore to me that there's never been anything between them."

"Who?"

"Edmond Dossin. It was just a game, but they carried on in such a way as to make anyone think they were together."

"Did you take the first car you found?"

"Yes. I didn't know whose it was. I've got a driver's license. I learned to drive because I thought it might help me get a job. But I've had no practice for a long time. It was raining . . . and coming back—"

"Just a moment . . . What did you do at the inn?"

"Nothing much. We danced a bit...It's a sort of roadhouse near the river."

"What's it called?"

"L'Auberge aux Noyés. It was shut when we got there, but we woke up the old lady and she came down—the girls too."

"Ah! There were girls!"

"Two. Eva and Clara. I can see what you're thinking. I thought so too at first, and Edmond tried to make out that they were pretty hot stuff, but I think they're respectable girls. Someone started the phonograph, and we danced. There wasn't much to drink—only beer and white wine. In the end we decided—"

"To finish up the party here!"

"Yes."

Outwardly Loursat's manner hadn't changed. But Emile felt that from now on he could say anything.

"I don't know how the accident happened. They'd given me cocktails at Joe's, and with the white wine on top of it...I jammed on the brakes, but it was too late. I can hardly remember the rest. Daillat took the wheel from me. I vomited, and when we got here, they had to help me upstairs."

"You went to sleep?"

"Yes. I woke up at four, when the doctor had already left. Edmond had gone too."

"What about Nicole?"

"She took care of me. The others had gone home, except Big Louie, who was in bed. He stared at me and I couldn't bear it. I kept on asking him to forgive me, and I asked Nicole too. I couldn't stop apologizing."

He got up, wondering whether it was wrong to talk as he had, whether the lawyer hadn't set a trap for him.

"If the police try to arrest me I'll kill myself."

His manner had changed abruptly. He had become hard again.

"I don't know why I came here. I suppose I'm only making a fool of myself... But before I go, may I see Nicole for a moment?"

"Sit down."

"I'm sorry, but I just can't keep still. It's been an awful day. Even now, my mother still knows nothing, though for the last two weeks she's been worrying about my coming home so late. Is it my fault if I . . ."

Did he want Loursat to buck him up? Not consciously, of course. But he was obsessed by the feeling that fate was somehow against him. A feeling common to self-absorbed young men. For that's what he was—self-absorbed. Even Nicole hardly existed except as the object of his love.

Had it been the same with Loursat when his wife left him?

Instinctively the lawyer reached for his glass. Why should this story of youthful folly have turned his thoughts inward? It was only now that it struck him that for the last hour he'd been thinking far more about himself than about Emile, Nicole, and the rest of their gang. Everything had got mixed up, as though there was some subtle connection between the present situation and what had happened long ago.

Yet there was no connection. Not even a resemblance. He hadn't been poor like Emile Manu or a Jew like Luska. He hadn't been delicate like his nephew Edmond. He hadn't been a frequenter of bars, nor had he passed off a cousin as his mistress.

Between him and these young people there wasn't merely the difference of a generation.

He was a solitary person! There! That was the truth he was looking for. As a young man he was already a lonely figure, too proud, perhaps. He had imagined a person could marry and still keep his solitude. Then one day he came home to an empty house.

But if there was no connection why should it bother him so to feel his scrubby beard on his chin?

Was he going to be forced to admit that he was suffering from a sensation that was uncommonly like humiliation?

Because he was forty-eight? Because he was dirty and slovenly? Because he drank?

No. He banished the thought with the reflection that the dinner bell had already rung twice and he was still sitting there with his visitor.

Steps approached along the passage. Someone touched the door handle, then decided to knock first.

"Who is it?"

"Me."

It was Nicole's gentle voice. Evidently Phine had informed her of Emile's visit.

Loursat got up and opened the door. She was very calm, her fair hair carefully done in a bun low on her neck.

"I hope I'm not interrupting you."

She went straight over to the young man, holding out her hand.

"Hello, Emile!"

"Hello. I've told your father everything."

"You were quite right."

It was only now, seeing those two together, that it occurred to Loursat that this boy was almost one of the family. They spoke to each other in such an easy, familiar way. Of course they would! Yet it hadn't struck him before, and, now that it did, it made him suddenly feel he was in the way.

It was to Emile that she asked: "Have you come to a decision?"

Loursat turned away, none too certain of being able to control his features. To cover his awkwardness he poured out another glass of wine. Why should his doing so disgust them? Didn't they drink? Didn't all those young people get together for that express purpose?

Steady now! Why should he be groping for excuses? Neither

of them had said a word, and if there was any look of disgust on their faces, he couldn't have seen it; he'd had his back to them.

The truth was...

Yes! That was it. That's what had been getting under his skin for the last hour—and perhaps for much longer—it was what had been nagging him and making him conscious of a sense of shame—he was alone.

Alone in time, alone in space, alone with a fat, ill-kept body, a scraggly beard, and great big liverish eyes, alone with his own thoughts that had long ago lost any zest or freshness, alone with his bottle of burgundy!

When he turned around on the others he had his surliest expression on his face.

"What are you waiting for?"

They didn't know, poor things! Emile was completely crestfallen and turned to Nicole for support.

"I'll show Emile out," she said, as though asking her father's approval.

He answered with a shrug of his shoulders.

And they hadn't gone ten yards along the passage before he stole over to the mantelpiece to look at himself in the glass.

"Is that you, Hector?"

There she was again, his pain of a sister, Marthe.

"I'm out of my mind with anxiety... Can you come over?... I simply must see you, if only for a few minutes... Charles is in Paris on business. I've tried to explain it all to him over the telephone, but he says he can't possibly return till tomorrow."

No response from Loursat. If his sister had been writhing in agony at his feet, it's doubtful if he'd have moved a muscle. As for that perfumed husband of hers, of course he couldn't come back till the next day. At that moment he'd be at a restaurant, dining in a private room with a beautiful woman!

"Listen!...Edmond hasn't come home yet...I hardly dare speak of this business over the telephone...Do you think it's safe?"

No answer.

"Don't you understand? He's still with the examining magistrate. Ducup rang me up a moment ago. I got Rogissart to ask him to keep me informed...It seems they're not yet done questioning him. Ducup didn't give any details, but from the hints he dropped it seems the case is much more serious than he thought at first, and it's going to be very difficult to hush it up...It's awful!...Oh, Hector! What are we to do?"

"Nothing."

"But, Hector..."

"What?"

"The whole thing happened in your house. Can't you see?...If only you'd kept an eye on Nicole. No—that wasn't what I meant. I'm so upset I hardly know what I'm saying... I've had to go to bed and send for the doctor."

Which she did in any case at least three times a week. Because she had the vapors, or because she was bored.

Illness to her was rather like burgundy was to her brother.

"Listen, Hector...Please make an effort and come and see me. Or, if you'd like to be very kind—"

"I'm never kind!"

"Don't, Hector! I know you don't really mean it. I can't go to the Palais de Justice in my state. Please go and get Edmond. That is, if they've finished with him. And then you can give us both your advice, particularly Edmond. I'm so afraid he'll say the wrong thing..."

Loursat answered at last, but only with a grunt that might equally well have meant yes or no. He put down the receiver and stood in the study looking around him. He frowned at the thought that strangers had invaded his sanctum.

Nicole had left the door open behind her. He went along

the passage and into the dining room to find her sitting in her usual place.

She jumped up at once as he entered, went over to the dumbwaiter. "The soup, Phine."

She avoided catching her father's eye. What would she be thinking about him? What would Emile have told her as they went down to the front door together? Had they kissed on parting?

He suddenly felt tired, washed out, rather, as he did in the mornings before the burgundy had begun to do its work.

"What's this soup supposed to be?"

"Pea soup."

"In that case why aren't there any croutons?"

Phine had forgotten them. They never had pea soup without croutons. He got quite worked up about it.

"Of course, if she spends half her day running around the town delivering notes, she can't have much time left for her cooking! And of course no one's thought of trying to get another housemaid."

Glancing up, he found her looking at him in amazement, and suddenly realized what he'd done. Not only had he said something, but he had actually betrayed an interest in what went on in the house. It was incredible!

"I've found one. She's starting tomorrow."

He was almost angry about it. So in spite of all that had happened, in spite of two hours' questioning by the examining magistrate, in spite of all those notes she'd had to write, in spite of having the police in the house, in spite of . . . in spite of everything, she had still found time to find a new maid!

"Where does she come from?" he asked mistrustfully.

"From the Convent."

"What? . . . What's that?"

"From the Convent. She's been a maid there. Now she has to leave because she's gotten engaged. Her name is Eléonore."

He couldn't very well lose his temper just because Nicole had engaged a new housemaid called Eléonore!

He went on with his soup. Halfway through, he began to notice the noise he made. No one ever made as much noise as that, except peasants or badly brought up children.

He shot a furtive glance at his daughter. If she heard, she wasn't taking any notice. But then, of course, she was used to it. She herself ate very properly. She did everything gracefully. As for what was going on in her mind, her thoughts were far away.

Quickly he looked down again, burying his face in his plate. What on earth had happened to him? It was preposterous. His face had become hot and if there weren't tears in his eyes they weren't far off. He must have looked a sight.

He finished his soup in record time, got to his feet, and made for the door.

"Father! Where are you going?"

She had always called him "Father," even as a little girl. Never "Papa."

He had thrown his napkin down on his chair. It wasn't till he reached the door that he could trust his voice sufficiently to mutter, "To your Aunt Marthe's."

And the extraordinary thing was, he was actually putting on his coat, ready to go!

5

HE HAD the impression of plunging back into life. He did things he had long since forgotten—or that he still did, only without realizing he was doing them—like turning up his overcoat collar, thrusting his hands deep in the pockets, and savoring the cold and the rain, the strange reflections of the sparkling streets.

As he passed other people he wondered where they were going. It was ages, years perhaps, since he'd been out at night. The lights in the rue d'Allier were different now. And the cinema was in a new spot.

Loursat walked quickly. His glances at the people and things about were still furtive, as if he was ashamed. But he hadn't entirely given in. He still grumbled to himself.

By the time he reached the glass and wrought-iron door of the Dossins' he had composed his features, and it was with the stoniest stare that he confronted the butler who tried to take his overcoat.

"Where is my sister?"

"Madame is in the *petit boudoir*. Will you come this way, Monsieur?"

Loursat had a good mind not to wipe his feet, just to protest against this white, showy hallway, to protest against its newness. He wiped them all the same, but the mere idea made him feel more like his usual self. Instead he lit a cigarette and threw the match on the floor.

"Oh, there you are, Hector! Come in! Shut the door, Joseph. If Monsieur Edmond comes back, tell him I'd like to see him at once."

Loursat was already bristling. He didn't like his sister. He never had. She'd never done anything to him, at any rate not since the days of their childhood. He couldn't stand her whimperings, her pale clothing, her soft elegance, or her husband, her house, or the way they set out to be stylish.

It wasn't jealousy. He had as much money as they had.

"Sit down, Hector. It really is kind of you to have come. Such a beastly night too. You didn't stop in at the Palais de Justice?... How much do you know about this dreadful business?... What did Nicole tell you? I suppose you've questioned her."

"I know nothing whatever," he answered grumpily, "except that they killed a man in my house."

Even as he spoke, his mind was elsewhere. He wondered why he harbored such resentment against the Dossins, and he was at a loss for a satisfactory answer. He despised them, of course, for their vanity, for the pretentious house that was their main obsession. And as for his brother-in-law, he had always regarded him as a perfect example of a fop.

"Really, Hector! You're surely not going to tell me it was the children who—"

"It looks like it, doesn't it?"

She got up from her sofa, forgetting her illness for a moment.

"Hector! You must be mad! Or is that your idea of a joke? You couldn't be so heartless. You know I'm at my wit's end. I asked you to come because I couldn't bear to be alone any longer, turning it over in my mind. And what do you do? You come running around here just for the cruel pleasure of telling me it's the children who—"

"You asked for the truth, didn't you?"

It was funny to think that if nothing had happened eighteen

years ago, his wife—for he would have a wife—would be about Marthe's age. Would she, as so many had done during the last ten years, would she have insisted on his building her a modern house?

That was hard to tell. He was thinking of so many things at once, as he watched his sister. He realized it was impossible to imagine what he would be now, married, possibly with more children, and he wondered what he would have done all those years.

"Listen, Hector! I know you're not always quite yourself. I can't tell whether you've been drinking or not, but really you must realize how serious this is. It's not the moment to shut yourself up in that dirty study of yours. You've got to do something. After all, the whole thing's your fault as much as anybody's. If you'd only brought up Nicole properly..."

"Look here, Marthe! Did you ask me around here just to preach to me?"

"I'm only trying to make you understand your duty. These children are young and irresponsible. Escapades are all very well up to a point, but in any ordinary house it would have been impossible for them to carry on as they've been doing. Sometimes I wonder whether you haven't known all the time what was going on. Now you're not lifting a finger. You're a lawyer. They may pity you at the Palais, but they still respect you, in spite of everything."

That's what she said: "In spite of everything"! And that they pitied him.

"I don't know whether Nicole takes after her mother."

"Marthe!"

"What?"

"Come here!"

"What for?"

So he could slap her face! Which he did, as astonished as she was by his sudden impulse.

"There! And now do you understand? Do I talk to you about your husband and the way he—"

He stopped short. Was it possible he could sink to that sort of argument, he who looked down on them all, he who had had the courage to live all alone for eighteen years in his corner, without caring a scrap for what they did, what they thought, what they said? Was it possible he could now start yelling at his sister, telling her that her own husband could do all his business in Moulins if it wasn't that he needed an excuse for going off and having a fling elsewhere? That the whole town knew about it, that she knew about it herself, and that her and her son's bad health was attributed to a certain old illness.

He looked for his hat, then remembered that the butler had taken it from him. Marthe had collapsed on her sofa weeping. And to think that these two people were in their forties, of an age, that is to say, when men and women are supposed to be sensible!

"You're going?"

"Yes."

"Won't you wait for Edmond?"

"Tell him to come and see me tomorrow morning—that is, if there's anything new."

"You've been drinking, haven't you?"

"No."

But he was irritated. And, when you really came to look at it, what irritated him was this question which had so suddenly reared itself up in front of him, and which, try as he might, he couldn't banish from his mind: "Why have I been living like a bear for eighteen years?"

Was it because Geneviève had gone off and left him high and dry? Though he had never admitted it, had her going really hurt him?

No. Hadn't his life as a student in Paris been very similar to what it was now? Hadn't he, by the age of twenty, already learned to stew in his own juice, with the poets and philosophers as only companions?

In the hall he snatched his hat from the butler's hands, then turned round to look hard into the latter's eyes. What was he thinking about all this?

The truth was he'd never tried to live—not in the ordinary sense of the word. That's what had struck him as he left home that evening, and the question was still preying on his mind. What was far more serious was that he now found he didn't want to go home.

Just as he had tried to fathom the butler's mind, so now he looked narrowly at the passersby, dark, mysterious figures who hurried past him.

What was it his sister had said about the people in the Palais de Justice? It can't have been true, surely? That they pitied him. They saw him as an oddball, as a sad character, maybe even as a failure.

And he despised them, the whole bunch of them, the Dossins, the Rogissarts, and all the others who thought they were living because they behaved just like each other.

His wet overcoat smelled of wool. Drops of rain trembled on the hairs of his beard. As he walked down the rue d'Allier, hugging the houses, it occurred to him that he must look just like an elderly gentleman sneaking off guiltily to a house of ill fame.

He passed a café. The windows were misty and the air inside full of tobacco smoke. He could, however, just make out some men playing billiards, others playing cards.

Loursat had never been able to do anything of that kind, had never been able to attach himself to any group of men, however small. He envied these men. He envied all those who had something to do or someplace to go to.

And Emile Manu too, a boy whose spirit vibrated like an overstrung wire. So tightly clenched that it was painful to observe the changing expression of his face—speaking of love, of death, challenging Loursat, begging him, watching him, only to threaten anew.

He must often have walked along that street at night with his friends—including Nicole! And day by day, hour by hour, they would be making up their own adventures as they went along.

While their parents, staying at home, pretended to be alive by decorating their houses, fretting about their servants, the quality of their cocktails, the success or otherwise of their dinner parties and bridge evenings.

Marthe could talk glibly about her son as though he was the most important thing in the world. But what did she really know about him? Nothing. No more than he, Loursat, knew about Nicole.

Reaching the Boxing Bar, he didn't hesitate a second. He barged through the door and stood for a moment looking around him while he shook the rain off his dripping overcoat.

The small room, softly lit by shaded lamps, was almost empty. A cat was sleeping on one of the tables. Near the bar, the proprietor was playing cards with two women who obviously belonged to the race that hibernated most of the day, coming out into the open after nightfall.

Loursat had never realized such people existed in Moulins. He sat down and crossed his legs. Joe promptly put down his cards and his cigarette and came over to him.

"What can I get you?"

He ordered a hot grog. Joe lit a gas ring behind the bar and put some water on to boil, at the same time glancing at his customer out of the corner of his eye. The two women watched him too as they sat with their cards in their hands and cigarettes between their lips. One of them seemed on the point of making advances, but Joe signaled to her that she'd be wasting her time.

It was peaceful there, with the cat purring in the silence. The street was quiet too, with hardly a soul about.

"I'd like a few words with you, Monsieur Loursat, if you don't mind," said Joe as he finally put the grog down beside the cat on the table.

"You know who I am, do you?"

"I guessed it was you when you came this afternoon. You see, I've heard..."

He threw a meaningful glance at the other table, which was doubtless the one at which the young people met.

"May I?"

He sat down in front of the lawyer, while the two women resigned themselves to a long wait.

"I'm surprised the police haven't yet been here to question me. Not that I've got anything to do with it. If there was anyone who tried to calm them down and give them a bit of advice, it was me. But you know what people are at that age."

He was quite at his ease and would no doubt have been just the same before the examining magistrate or even giving evidence in court.

"It goes without saying that they made themselves out to be much worse than they really were. If you ask me, it's all because of movies. All that gangster stuff. Puts ideas in their heads. But when you know them like I do you can see it's only playacting. Again and again I've tried to throw cold water on their schemes."

He turned toward the two women.

"You can back me up there, can't you? Time and again I've said they'd only get themselves into trouble and most likely me too.

"When they leave this place, it's generally because I've refused to serve them any more liquor. Then the other day they brought in this new guy, Emile. He'd got no money to speak of, but he wanted to stand a round of drinks like the others—wanted it so bad that he asked me to lend him twenty francs against his watch. I didn't want the watch, but I let him have the money.

"You understand, at my age..."

He was evidently intrigued by Loursat, who didn't quite fit in with what he'd heard. What had those kids said about him? Most likely they had depicted the lawyer as a broken-down old man, sodden with drink.

With an almost familiar smile Joe went on. "What I could never make out was how you never came to hear anything. When you think they were whooping it up and dancing till five in the morning. At times I even wondered..."

"What'll you have?"

Joe winked. With only a little more encouragement he'd have given Loursat a dig in the ribs. And the latter wouldn't have minded at all. On the contrary!

"A *menthe* for me, thanks. And what about you? The same again?"

As Joe passed the women's table, he gave them a meaningful look. One of them got up, giving a yank to her dress, and, through it, to her drawers, which had ridden up between her buttocks.

"I think I'll have a stroll outside," she announced.

A minute or two later the other followed suit, and the two men were left alone, Loursat and the boxer, in the soothing quiet of the bar.

"Do you want me to tell you what I think? After all, I've probably seen more of them than anybody. I'm not suggesting they took me into their confidence. I didn't want it. All the same, I couldn't help hearing things, noticing things—could I? For instance, take the young lady, Mademoiselle Nicole. I wouldn't mind betting there's never been anything between her and Monsieur Edmond. In fact I'll go further than that. I'm convinced Monsieur Edmond isn't really interested in girls at all. I've known fellows like that. And what with him being the weak type, I'd swear he was afraid. That's the way it is with timid fellows, they talk big.

"As for the little guy..."

The little guy was Emile Manu, and Loursat was not displeased to hear him spoken of in a tone that was almost affectionate.

"That very first evening, if I'd had half a chance, I'd have taken him aside and warned him not to get mixed up with the crowd. It's the same with that other one, the one they call Luska, who works all day long on the sidewalk outside Prisunic. You see what I'm driving at, don't you? It's all very well for guys like Monsieur Edmond and that other one—what's his name? son of a businessman, came in a few times—they can get up at any hour of the day. Besides, if there's any trouble, their parents are always there.

"But these underfed boys—you've only got to take one look at them to know that at home they count the money sou by sou.

"And of course, if they're poor, they're all the more anxious to put up a good show. That kid Emile had never had a thing to drink before...

"I didn't see them the next day, but the day after that Monsieur Edmond dropped in. He told me they'd run over a man who was being looked after in your house.

" 'If you take my advice,' I told him, 'you'll go to the police and...' "

Sometimes Loursat had to make quite an effort to persuade himself he was really there, listening greedily to Joe's story and even piping up to ask questions.

"Did you know Big Louie?"

"Not personally. But I'd heard about him. Enough to know straight off what his little game was. A pretty nasty customer, I'd bet. These country louts often are. They can strangle a child in the woods, or beat up an old woman for her savings. I don't need to tell you about that sort of thing. You're a lawyer and probably know more about it than I do.

"The mistake they made was not to drive straight on and leave him lying in the road. When he found himself in a grand house with a young lady waiting on him hand and foot, he naturally thought he'd stumbled on a little gold mine. Make them pay through the nose—that's what he'd do! Only, he didn't bargain for what they were going to do to him."

Joe held out his packet of cigarettes, as to an old pal, then gave the lawyer a light.

"All I can tell you about it is that the whole business lay pretty heavy on their chests. They didn't meet as much as before and when they did they weren't the same. No more shouting and laughing. They talked in whispers and shut up if I came near. Don't think I'm complaining about that. It was no concern of mine.

"I've no idea how they thought of getting rid of him. After all, they couldn't very well leave the corpse in one of your bedrooms, could they? And to get it down to the river—a job like that's not so easy.

"Look! I may as well tell you that only today Monsieur Edmond came here. At about twelve o'clock. He'd just come away from class. He was paler than ever and he had bags under his eyes. For a moment I wondered whether I ought to give him any alcohol.

" 'Someone's been acting stupid,' he snarled. 'Those idiots! They go and take everything we say in deadly earnest.'

"I looked at him and said nothing. I thought there was more, but he was in a rush.

" 'We're in it now, right up to the neck. Heaven knows how my mother'll take it.' "

Phine called Emile "Monsieur" as a term of affection. Joe called Edmond "Monsieur," possibly because he was the son of a rich manufacturer, or perhaps because he was more or less the leader of the group of young people and the one who most often paid.

Loursat was as absorbed by the story as by a book. Not a word was lost on him, not the most trifling detail.

Joe was by now so used to this man with the big head and glaucous eyes that he went over to the bar for some more drinks, saying simply, "It's my round."

No less simply, Loursat accepted.

"This afternoon," began Joe again, "I thought you were going to question me. Then I realized that, seeing the sort of people involved, the case would be hushed up. All the same, it doesn't look like it. I hear that Monsieur Edmond has been summoned to the Palais de Justice."

"Who told you?"

"The one who's in the bank. What's his name? Destrivaux or something like that. I never could understand what made him join up with a gang like that. Do you know him?"

"No."

"A tall, thin kid. Of course most of them are a bit weedy at that age. Except the butcher's son ... But that Destrivaux, he's skinnier than them all. And such a proper young man, what with his spectacles and his hair parted in the middle. Shy as a girl too. To tell the truth, I never could stomach him. It seems his father's been chief cashier in the same bank for thirty years. And you know what banks are like! If you're not a hundred percent respectable, out you go. So you can just imagine the state he's in now with a storm like this blowing up."

"You mean the father?"

"No. The boy. He came around here on his bicycle after the bank shut. Wanted to find out if I knew anything. Seems he'd had a note from somebody!"

Of course! From Nicole. She hadn't left anyone out and Phine had had to trot all over town.

"He could hardly face going home. He asked me a lot of questions, casual like, as though it was just for the sake of saying something. But I could see what was at the back of his mind all right. Wanted to know if it was easy for the police to find someone in Paris. I told him to run off was the worst thing he could do—that it would only get him an extra two or three months."

Loursat listened with intense interest; was that why he suddenly felt so anxious?

"I suppose you'll be taking the case on yourself," he probed. "They say you don't often appear in court, but when you do you make them all sit up. Anyhow, if you want me to give evidence . . . I've had a bit of trouble myself in my day, but I have a clean record now. They're not even allowed to bring it up!"

For a while now Loursat had thought it was time for him to be going. Only, he couldn't tear himself away. He was like a child fascinated by a story and dreading the moment when it comes to an end.

"Do you know the inn they went to, the Auberge aux Noyés?" he asked, resisting the temptation to have a fourth glass of grog.

His eyes hurt him. He was flushed. Tonight he must at all costs keep within bounds.

"It's not much of a place. They seemed to have the idea it was pretty hot. But then, they were like that. For instance, if a pal of mine was to come in and say something to me in a low voice they'd straight away jump to the conclusion he belonged to the underworld. They even got the idea the police were on their track. I used to have to go and look out into the street to see there were no cops around! I think they'd all bought revolvers, though I don't suppose for a moment they could use them—"

"Well! One of them seems to have!" put in Loursat.

In his house too! And, apart from Angèle and probably Phine, nobody in the whole town—he less than anyone—had ever suspected that a crowd of young people little more than children had kicked over the traces and were leading a riotous life on the fringes of everyone else's.

Edmond was his mother's darling, and with her he was as gentle as a girl. Then, when others went to bed...

"How much do I owe you?"

"Sixteen francs. That's charging you the same as I charge them. I make a special price for regular customers... Do you think the fellow that—that did it will get away with extenuating circumstances?"

He spoke almost like a professional, avoiding certain unpleasant words.

"The courts have been coming down on that sort of thing pretty heavily lately. The other day at Rouen a kid of nineteen was sentenced to death."

At the corner of the street, Loursat passed one of the two women. She was sauntering up and down on her high heels, holding an umbrella. "Goodnight, dear!" she said casually.

Even now he couldn't make up his mind to go home to settle down into the room that had engulfed him for the last eighteen years. Reaching the place d'Allier he acted on the spur of the moment, hailing a passing taxi.

"Do you know an inn called the Auberge aux Noyés at Les Coqueteaux?"

"Out toward the old post office?"

"I think so."

"You want me to take you there?"

The driver, who had the air of a comfortable family man, looked critically at the lawyer, but after a moment's hesitation threw open the door.

"It'll be sixty francs, there and back."

How long had it been since Loursat had been in a taxi, particularly at night? He hardly recognized the route out of town, past the cemetery, past the new section where Emile and his mother lived.

"There's something burning," said the driver, turning around.

Loursat had dropped a cigarette butt on the carpet. He put it out with his heel.

"You know, you run a good chance of finding the place closed and everyone gone to bed."

It had once been a private car, and there was no partition between the driver and the back seat. The driver would have liked to chat. The windshield wiper flicked to and fro, with an irritating sound. Occasionally they passed the headlights of oncoming cars.

"Let's see! I think this is where we turn. I don't come this way very often."

At the end of a bumpy road, about two hundred meters from a farm with whitewashed walls, they saw the reflection of the muddy-banked river. There was the two-story house, all lit up.

"Aha! Are you going to be long?"

"I don't think so."

He had read endless books, he had digested them, pondered over them. Day by day, year after year, he had turned over all the problems of human beings. Yet there were all sorts of simple things he didn't know how to do: he couldn't even walk into an inn and sit down at a table.

As a matter of fact he hadn't even known that such places as this existed. Awkwardly he sidled in, with a mistrustful look in his eye.

Yet it was an ordinary place, if anything a bit cleaner than most country inns. The bar was made of pine and the walls were done with oil paint plastered over with liquor advertisements. But in spite of the line of tables and the row of bottles behind the bar, the feeling you got was somehow not that of a public place. There was a calmness and intimacy about it like that of a family kitchen, in a farmhouse for instance. Perhaps the cream-colored curtains had something to do with it.

At one of the tables a man was sitting, a middle-aged man

whom Loursat took to be a grain merchant or poultry dealer. He must be the man who owned the truck Loursat had seen outside. A girl was sitting by his side. The lawyer might have been wrong, but as he entered he thought he saw the man quickly withdraw his hand from her lap.

Now they both stared at him, either with curiosity or annoyance, probably both. As for him, he sat down at another table after once more shaking the rain off his overcoat.

"What would you like?" asked the girl, coming over to him.

"A grog."

"I'm afraid the stove's out, and we haven't got gas here... Perhaps you'd like a glass of rum?"

"All right."

She opened a door at the far end of the room and called out, "*Maman*!... Eva!"

Then she went back where she'd been sitting, put her elbows on the table, and tried to summon a smile. She succeeded fairly well for someone who was almost dropping with sleep.

"What did you answer?" she asked, resuming the conversation at the point where Loursat had interrupted it.

The door at the far end had been left ajar. Behind it, he could clearly see a face lit up by the light from the room. It belonged to a woman of about forty, who had already done her hair in curlers for the night.

She was peering through at him, but, catching his eye, she quickly drew back. She must have gone upstairs again, as he could hear two people moving about overhead.

It was five minutes before Eva appeared. She was so like the other girl that anyone could tell at a glance they were sisters. As she came up to Loursat, he could see by her eyes that she had already been asleep.

"Have you ordered anything?"

"A rum," called out the other.

"A large?"

He answered yes. It was all extremely interesting, he was determined not to miss anything. He tried to picture the group of young people and Nicole...Emile Manu, who'd gone out that night for the first time and gotten drunk.

They were watching him, trying to guess what he was doing there. When Eva brought the rum, she didn't have the nerve to sit at his table. For a moment she hovered nearby, and then finally went and stood behind the bar.

The grain merchant took out his wallet. "How much?"

"Are you going already?"

He glanced in Loursat's direction, as if as to say, "Too much of a crowd here tonight!"

She tried to coax him into staying, then went to the door to see him off. Outside there was a silence before they said goodnight. That must have been a kiss, a caress.

When she came back indoors, she seemed dull and listless. She made an effort to brighten up, however. "Nasty weather!" she said to Loursat.

Then: "You don't come from these parts, do you? Are you traveling on business?"

They weren't bad-looking, either of them. Rather pretty, in fact. But they lacked any real freshness or sparkle.

"I'm thirsty—Eva! Buy me a lemonade, Monsieur?"

He had the impression the mother came down to peep through the door from time to time. It made him feel he'd been caught doing something wrong.

"Cheers!...You'll stand Eva a drink too, won't you?"

So that in the end all three were sitting around the table in strained silence. The two girls carried on a whole conversation by the exchange of meaningful looks. Perceiving it, Loursat felt more and more ill at ease.

"How much will that be?"

"Nine francs, fifty. I'm afraid I haven't got any change... Thanks...I suppose you've got a car."

He found his taxi turned the other way around, ready to drive off.

"Nothing doing, was there? I warned you it wasn't much of a place, didn't I? You can have a drink and a bit of a laugh with them, and you think you're getting on fine...but as for the rest..."

Mixed with Loursat's embarrassment was a certain satisfaction at being taken for a man who'd drive to the end of the world on a foul night in search of a place where he could amuse himself with girls.

For some obscure reason the feeling was connected with his sister Marthe. He could see her, in her pale green dress, getting slapped. He'd have liked her to be there with him now.

"Do many people come here?" he asked, leaning forward to catch the driver's reply.

"Some regular customers, but I doubt if there'd be more than a handful of them. Mostly young people who want to go wild and don't have the nerve to do it in town."

There wasn't a light showing in the new quarter with unfinished streets where Emile Manu lived. At the Boxing Bar, on the other hand, there were two silhouettes behind the curtains.

"Where shall I drop you?"

"It doesn't matter. Here, at the next corner."

Like someone who can't bear the end of a party, he wanted to draw out his evening, stopping at times to listen to the sound of distant footsteps.

In the street, he passed, one by one, the big houses that were much the same as his. He hated them—them and the people inside them—just as he hated his sister, Dossin, Rogissart, his wife, Ducup, and a host of others. There was no end to the list. People who had done him no harm whatever, whose only offense was to be on the other side of the barricade. A place, in fact, where he might have been himself if his wife hadn't run off with someone named Bernard, if he hadn't spent eighteen years entombed in his study, and if he hadn't discovered, beneath the many superimposed layers of propriety that formed the social texture of the town, another, hitherto unsuspected, world: where Nicole held her own with Ducup and sent notes all around town; where Joe the Boxer bought him a drink; where Emile Manu flared up or was on the verge of tears; where Edmond Dossin caused problems for his respectable mother and his fop of a father; where that young bank clerk, son of a model employee, wanted to run away to Paris; and where Luska sold shoes on the sidewalk outside Prisunic.

As he mused, he'd instinctively been feeling for his key. He tried one pocket after another, then came to a halt, interrupting his train of thought to realize he'd gone out without it.

Phine would never dream of coming down to open the door. She was much too scared. And Nicole would be fast asleep.

Suddenly he remembered the back door, and went around into the little side alley to see whether it was still being left unlocked.

His face lit up as the door opened. It was rather fun going in that way. It gave him the feeling of being almost *one of them*!

6

LYING in bed, with his bushy whiskers quivering as he snored, he must have seemed enormous and wicked—the big bad ogre. And Phine, who'd just tiptoed in, was the Fairy Godmother, dashing hither and thither to save her Little Princess, delivering letters down the rue d'Allier, to Luska, Destrivaux, Dossin—an ill-tempered fairy to everyone else, but unfailingly good to her dear one.

Loursat couldn't help smiling. This image had come to mind as Phine stood by his bed looking at him curiously. Who knows, perhaps, on mornings like this, as he lay there inert, at her mercy, she had fantasized about taking her revenge on him with something stronger than a sour look.

He realized it was raining outside. And he had forgotten to close the shutters of his study the previous evening.

"What is it, Phine?"

"A letter."

"You're waking me up for a letter?"

"A gendarme brought it around, saying it was urgent."

It was not till he had fully regained his consciousness that he noticed the change in Phine's demeanor. She was lifeless and despondent, and her private war with the master of the house appeared for the moment to be suspended.

She stood waiting for him to open the letter, then asked, "Is it bad news?"

"The prosecutor asks me to go to the Palais de Justice this morning."

She had never known him to get up from his bed and dress so quickly.

"Is Nicole up?" he called to her as he buttoned up his trousers.

"She went out some time ago."

"What time is it?"

"Almost eleven. It wasn't ten when she went out."

"Do you know where she went?"

There was definitely a truce between them, though Phine remained on her guard. She hesitated before answering, finally deciding that he'd better know.

"Monsieur Emile's mother came to fetch her."

And severely, almost as though it was his fault, she added, "Monsieur Emile was arrested this morning."

So while he had been sweating and snoring in bed...He looked out of the window at the gray sky and the shiny wet sidewalk. Anyhow, here it was—another dismal rainy day. The milk-girl, who was just then passing on her round, was protecting herself as best as she could with a sack over her head and shoulders. He imagined the streets in the new district near the cemetery. What was the name of Emile's street? Oh, yes. Rue Ernest-Voivenon! Not even the name of a local celebrity. Merely the landlord's!

He thought of the people who lived there. Hundreds and hundreds of them getting up in the dark on winter mornings to hurry off—most of them on bicycles—to their work in town.

That meant the police had to make an early start too if they wanted to catch Emile Manu before he left home to go to his bookshop. There would have been a policeman posted at the corner of the street. Loursat could imagine the neighbors peering through their lace curtains so as not to be seen themselves.

Mme Manu would be getting his breakfast ready, no doubt, as he got dressed.

But Phine hadn't finished her story, and it was once more in a tone of reproach that she went on. "He tried to commit suicide."

"What? He tried to kill himself? With what?"

"A revolver."

"Did he hurt himself?"

"No. The thing wouldn't go off. When he heard the police talking to his mother in the hall, he ran to the attic, and that's where..."

Loursat could just imagine it: the imitation marble that lined the walls, the straw mats in front of every doorway. And in barge a couple of burly policemen cluttering up the place and leaving muddy footprints on the linoleum.

Phine came back into the bedroom to make the bed. Loursat put on his overcoat, which was still damp from the previous night, and his bowler hat. Outside the damp air was piercingly cold, like that in a cavern. Nasty drips fell from the cornices, catching you unawares.

So Mme Manu's first reaction was to come and find Nicole! Why? To heap her with blame? Hardly. Though in her heart of hearts she could hardly fail to hold the girl responsible. Wasn't Nicole older than her boy, richer, and better off?

The shame she must have felt that morning, going out to brave the eyes of her neighbors! Crying, no doubt, as she walked, and talking to herself, perhaps rehearsing what she would say to Nicole.

Then they went off together to defend Emile, leaving Phine to guard the sleeping ogre.

Loursat began to understand the note he had received. It wasn't an official summons.

Dear friend,

It appears to be impossible to get you on the telephone. Would you please come around to the Palais as soon as you possibly can?

I shall be waiting for you,

—Gérard Rogissart.

Loursat noted that Rogissart had omitted the standard friendly closing to the letter.

It didn't occur to the lawyer to adopt any particular attitude as he entered the Palais de Justice, yet, as he went through the great hall swarming with people—plaintiffs, defendants, witnesses, and those in robes, his colleagues of the bar—he acted, in spite of himself, like someone about to do battle. His shoulders rounded, his hands thrust deep in his pockets, he rushed up the staircase to the prosecutor's office.

On the floor above, the first thing he saw was a couple of women sitting on a bench, their backs against the green-painted wall. The first, in black clothes and button boots, was Mme Manu, Emile's mother, who clutched a handkerchief in her hand. Her neighbor, who of course was none other than Nicole, was holding that hand in a way that suggested sympathy rather than affection.

Mme Manu wasn't crying now, though she had certainly done so. In her eyes was an expression of tragic bewilderment. Others were waiting too, an old man on the same bench, a hoodlum between two gendarmes on the next.

Pretending not to see the two women, Loursat sailed straight past, making for Rogissart's door, which he opened without knocking.

He had avoided a painful scene in the corridor—that was one good thing. In the room two men were standing at the window, silhouetted against the light. At his entrance, they swung around together.

"Ah! At last!" said Rogissart going over to his desk and sitting down.

The other figure was Ducup, looking more like a rat than ever. Loursat noted that each had placed himself so as not to be near him, so as not to have to shake hands with him.

"Sit down, Hector...I suppose we've dragged you out of bed."

Roggisart couldn't very well help calling Loursat by his Christian name since they were cousins and had spent a good deal of their childhood together. To prevent the greeting from sounding too friendly, however, he added the remark about bed, which was intentionally spiteful. At the same time he started fiddling with various papers, as though to color the interview with a touch of officialdom.

As for Ducup, he remained standing. By the look on his face, he knew what was coming and was determined to enjoy it to the full.

"I am very concerned about what's happened," began the prosecutor. "It's really a most deplorable business from beginning to end. Indeed I've been so worried about it that I—but I must ask you to keep this strictly to yourself—that I did something I've never done before in the whole of my career: rang up the Ministry of Justice to ask for advice."

Where would Emile be now? Was he already locked up in a cell? Or perhaps sitting, like those two women, on a bench in a dismal corridor, waiting to be interrogated, except that, unlike them, he would be closely guarded.

"You understand, of course, that I didn't summon you here officially. I may have to do that later. Meanwhile we thought—Ducup and I—that we ought to ask you to help us, or at any rate to explain to you how matters stand.

"Yesterday Ducup questioned young Dossin at length, and I was present myself part of the time. You know the boy of course, since he's a nephew of yours.

"I must confess I couldn't help being sorry for him. I'd met him before, naturally, since I've often had dinner with his parents. He'd always struck me as a bit delicate, with something soft about him, almost effeminate, yet I'd never have thought he was so highly strung. It was painful to look at. Indeed he was in such a state of nerves that I began to wonder whether I oughtn't to call a doctor.

"However, Ducup handled him with the utmost tact and in the end the boy was speaking freely..."

Loursat's reaction to this opening speech came as a complete surprise to the two others. He got up from his chair, took off his overcoat, and hung it up in a cupboard which he knew had some hooks in it. He went back for the pack of cigarettes he had left in his coat pocket, then, resuming his seat, crossed his legs, took out a notebook, and laid it on his knee, his right hand brandishing a pencil.

"May I?"

For a moment or two there was a silence. Both Rogissart and Ducup were somewhat taken aback by Loursat's attitude. They glanced at each other, not without a touch of uneasiness, wondering whether they ought to regard it as a threat.

"You know, I suppose, what I have to tell you, what everyone will know in a few hours—it's impossible to hush up a case involving a death. The minister is of my opinion: In this affair, Edmond Dossin has been only an accessory, and, to a certain extent, a victim. I can appreciate now how impressionable he is.

"A group of young people has been frequenting a somewhat doubtful bar near the marketplace, young people of family, and some others: the butcher's son, the son of a—"

"I know," Loursat interrupted.

"In that case you must have discovered that your daughter was more or less the central figure, that your house was their headquarters. I am very sorry to have to say so, not only for your sake, but for the sake of us all. The scandal will hit many of the best families in the town. It will be difficult, in open court, for the jury to believe that a whole band of young people could engage in midnight debaucheries under your roof, even dance to a phonograph, without the master of the house being aware of it."

Ducup, playing the part of the audience, nodded his head.

"Things probably wouldn't have gone any further, if a new-comer hadn't joined the group just under three weeks ago. This Emile Manu proposed stealing a car the very first night—bor-rowing, if you prefer—so that the evening festivities could be continued at a country inn some distance from the town.

"As regards the subsequent events, Edmond Dossin seems to have been the only one to display some sense of responsibility, since it was he who went to fetch Dr. Matray, asking for strict confidentiality."

It was strange that the words should evoke memories of Loursat's childhood, certain facial expressions and attitudes of his sister Marthe. He thought he could still hear her say, when their parents discovered something wrong: "Hector did it!"

Even in those days she had been delicate, so highly strung that no one would cross her. This didn't prevent her from giv-ing her brother a look that said: "There you are! I can do just as I like with them! You're in for it again!"

The prosecutor arranged his features into a suitable expres-sion to say, "There's an aspect of the case we've been obliged to investigate, distasteful though it is, as it is bound to come up in court. I refer to the relations between Edmond and Nicole. I am persuaded, however, that the boy was telling me the truth when he assured me that their conduct in this respect was merely a game and that there was really nothing behind it at all . . . I'm very sorry to have to touch on matters of this sort. I do not think the same is true as far as Manu is concerned. The presence of the injured man gave him an excellent excuse to go there every night.

"And I have every reason to believe that the patient was not without influence upon the young man. I suppose you'll be ready to admit that I have some experience in criminal matters. Manu falls into a definite category—the overexcitable, hotheaded kind, who may equally well become saints or jailbirds, depending on whether they come under good influence or bad.

"Where others are merely playing, he takes it seriously.

"I'm not suggesting that Edmond said so in so many words, but it was impossible to draw any other conclusion from what he told us.

"I have no doubt whatever that the addition of Manu to the group effected a profound change in its activities. Whereas so far their misdeeds had amounted to no more than youthful escapades, they now began to talk of crime, even to the extent of toying with the idea of burglary.

"Don't think I'm ignoring Big Louie's influence, which was no doubt considerable, notwithstanding his being laid up in bed. We've had a good deal of information about him and it's all as bad as could be.

"Incidentally, it may interest you to learn that during the weeks he was in your home, Big Louie sent off several money orders, amounting in all to two thousand six hundred francs, to a girl now living in a village in Normandy who has had three children by him. The money orders have been traced—that's how we've discovered her whereabouts. I've sent an order through to Honfleur that she be questioned. If necessary I'll have her brought here.

"This brings us to what I believe is the truth. Ducup takes the same view as I do, and I'd like to say in passing that he has conducted his inquiry with a scrupulousness and a tact for which we all of us have reason to be grateful."

Loursat coughed. That was all, but he coughed, then he continued to sketch on a page of his notebook.

"Under the influence of Big Louie, Manu must no doubt have committed a number of misdemeanors, for in Edmond's view that money could only have come from him. Did he become frightened? Did Big Louie become too demanding? Probably. In any case the latter seems to have decided to eliminate him."

And as if Loursat didn't know it, the prosecutor added, "I've had the young man arrested this morning. He is here. There should be a hearing in a matter of weeks."

With that, he got up from his desk and walked over to the window.

"It is most regrettable that your daughter should have thought fit to come rushing here with the boy's mother. They're outside in the corridor. You must have seen them . . . Ducup has done his best. He took Nicole quietly aside and tried to make her understand the impropriety of her action, but to no avail . . . Under these conditions, if I am obliged to charge the boy, it will be difficult for people to see why . . ."

Loursat looked up.

" . . . Why you don't arrest Nicole too!" he said as coolly as could be.

"We haven't reached that point yet, I'm thankful to say. All the same I thought I'd better send for you. Your position, in our town, is somewhat special. We all respect you, we know your talents, and the rest we put down to certain unfortunate circumstances in which you have all our sympathy, and accordingly we are only anxious to make light of those eccentricities which . . ."

The words suddenly made Loursat realize he hadn't had a single glass of wine that morning!

"There's no need to go into specifics . . . though no doubt it would have been better if Nicole had been brought up differently, or been supervised like other girls."

Once again Loursat coughed. The prosecutor and the examining magistrate exchanged glances that were almost anxious. Had they expected him to sit there meekly listening with a hang-dog air to a well-earned sermon, like the broken-down drunk they took him to be?

"Have you got any evidence against Emile Manu?"

"A strong presumption, at any rate. He was in your house when the crime was committed. Nicole admits that. She seems to glory in the fact that this young man had spent the evening in her bedroom."

If he wasn't getting the picture, well then, they'd have to put it a bit more bluntly.

"Are you beginning to understand?"

"I'd like to be present when you question Emile Manu."

"Are you undertaking his defense?"

"Perhaps. I don't know yet."

"Listen, Hector..."

Rogissart made a sign to Ducup, who walked rather awkwardly out of the room, and began speaking in a low voice, "We're relatives. My wife is very upset over this affair. Your sister Marthe telephoned me this morning. Edmond is in bed. They're worried about his condition; he's in a serious nervous state. Charles dashed back from Paris this morning. I've had a word with him too. I need hardly tell you he is furious with you. Just this morning everything was set... When they went to arrest Manu this morning he tried to shoot himself. Either the gun jammed or he forgot to remove the safety in his panic... Or else it was all an act—that's not impossible. Don't think I'm being cynical, Hector. That might well have been the most merciful solution for the boy himself, to say nothing of all the trouble it would have avoided for others.

"After all, his attempt to take his life as good as proves his guilt, doesn't it?

"But just suppose that, to avenge himself, he dragged your daughter, Edmond, and all the rest down with him?

"You'll agree that the whole town, your relatives, and your friends have respected your wish to be alone for such a long time, and that everyone has kept silent about your peculiarities and extravagances.

"This is serious, Hector—very serious."

Loursat lit a cigarette.

"Suppose you call Manu in," he suggested.

He was moved all the same. Not in the way the others might have imagined. For if a comparison had to be found for his feelings it would be to those of a young man waiting at his first rendezvous with a girl.

He was waiting for Emile Manu! He was dying to see him! He envied Phine, who had run around town distributing Nicole's notes. He envied his daughter sitting on a bench in the company of thieves and gendarmes, braving the stares, inquisitive, disdainful, or pitying, of passersby, as she did her best to console a distracted mother.

Something unexpected had happened to him, something shattering. He had come out of his lair, into the street, into the town.

He had watched Nicole at the table, Nicole, who, lacking a maid, had gotten up to get the plates from the dumbwaiter, and put them on the table without saying a word.

He had looked at Emile too. He had listened to Joe, the boxer. He had gone out there, to that inn with the two daughters, the mother in her dressing gown surveying them through a half-open door.

He had wanted to . . .

It was so difficult to form an idea of what he wanted, much less to express it in words. He wasn't used to it, and he was afraid of seeming foolish.

"Wanted to live," for instance. No. He couldn't bring himself to say that. "Wanted a fight," perhaps. That was about it. He wanted to let off steam, wanted to break out—break out of that stuffy overheated den of his, whose walls were lined with books, whose door was padded to shut out all intruding sounds.

And to rush out...

To sit down to dinner with Nicole and say in an offhand way, "Don't be afraid."

So long as she understood that he was on their side, was with them and not the others, that he was with his daughter, with Phine, with Emile, and with that piano-teaching mother of his!

And he hadn't had so much as one glass of burgundy! He felt heavy, but solid, in control.

He waited with almost breathless impatience, straining his ears for the sounds in the corridor. First came the gendarmes' heavy footsteps, then a stifled cry from Mme Manu and the sounds of something like a scuffle as she threw herself at her boy and had to be dragged away.

At last the doors opened and a man in plain clothes looked in inquiringly. At a sign from the prosecutor he vanished, reappearing the next moment with Emile Manu in tow.

It was the pompous voice of Rogissart, who undertook pilgrimages to Lourdes and Rome with yearly regularity in the hope of one day becoming a father.

"The examining magistrate is going to ask you a few questions. Your answers will not be recorded as this is not a formal interrogation. You may therefore speak quite freely, and I cannot impress upon you too strongly that your best course will be to..."

Immediately on entering, the young man's quick, darting eyes had sought Loursat, and remained fixed on him until the prosecutor was halfway through his little speech.

And Loursat had recoiled, wounded. Yes, wounded, for he

could read in that look an accusation, that Emile held him responsible for his present plight, for his mother's misery.

"I came to you in all frankness," he seemed to be saying. "I opened my heart to you, I almost wept on your shoulder. And now I find you here among the ranks of my enemies. It's you who had me arrested, you who..."

He was left standing in the middle of the room. He wasn't tall. His right knee was muddy. His hands were trembling, though he was making an effort to keep himself under control.

And Loursat envied him! Not so much to be eighteen as to be capable of despair and to be there, head swimming, to feel his world turned upside down, to know that his mother was in tears, that Phine had adopted him and only him, that he was the only one Nicole truly loved.

They loved him! Unconditionally. With a devotion that was absolute. The world might torture, condemn, and finally execute him, yet these women would never lose faith.

He had turned away from Loursat now, and he gazed intently at Ducup, who took his place at the desk while the prosecutor paced up and down the room.

"As Monsieur le Procureur has just explained to you, this is not—"

"I didn't kill Big Louie." The words seemed to burst out as though forced from him by an irresistible pressure.

"I must beg you not to interrupt me. As Monsieur le Procureur has just explained to you, this is not so much an official interrogation as a private interview. Accordingly—"

"I didn't kill him."

The boy put out his hand and gripped the wooden desk, with its green leather top. Perhaps because he was shaking? That desk, that livid window—opening onto a day that no one else knew anything about, that he alone could see.

"I won't go to prison. I—"

He swung around and glared at Loursat as though seized by

a wild desire to go for him tooth and nail. "It's him, isn't it? He's the one who—"

"I'm asking you to calm yourself."

The prosecutor put his hand on the boy's shoulder. Loursat hung his head, overcome by a vague sense of shame, shame at being what he was, shame at not having known how to win Emile's trust.

Nor Nicole's either, nor Phine's, nor, in all probability, Madame Manu's.

He was an enemy!

Ducup seemed at a loss to know what to say and it was Rogissart who went on: "It was I who requested Maître Loursat to be present at this interview, considering the peculiar situation in which he has been placed...Those are matters, however, which I can hardly expect you to understand. You are young and impulsive. You have acted thoughtlessly, and unfortunately—"

"Do you really think I killed Big Louie?"

Emile was really trembling now, but Loursat saw it was not from fear, but from a sort of rage at his own impotence, his inability to make himself understood, his isolation in face of the cunning processes of the law, hounded by two magistrates while Loursat looked on like some large, evil animal lurking in the corner.

"It's not true! I admit I stole the car, but I didn't do it alone. We were all in it together."

The contortions of the boy's features were horrible to watch. It was as though he was weeping without actual tears.

"You've no right to pick on me as if I was the only one. I didn't fire that shot, I tell you...I didn't—"

"Gently! Gently!"

The prosecutor was alarmed. In spite of the padded door, Emile's voice must have been audible in the corridor outside.

"They even had to bring me away in handcuffs, as though I was a common—"

To everyone's surprise, Ducup suddenly made up his mind to intervene. Rapping on the desk with a paperknife he shouted, "Silence!"

So unexpected was his outburst that Emile stopped dead, gaping at the examining magistrate with almost comic bewilderment.

"You're here to answer our questions, not to indulge in a melodramatic performance. I really must insist on a certain decorum."

Emile swayed, unsteady on his thin legs. Beads of sweat stood on his upper lip and temples. Seen from the back, his neck was like a chicken's.

"So you do not deny having borrowed—you see I'm putting it very mildly—a car to drive your companions to the country, a car, to be exact, that belonged to the mayor's secretary. Owing to your inexperience as a driver or to your state of intoxication, you met with an accident."

Emile frowned, creasing his forehead into three deep lines. He was unable to grasp what was said to him. He heard all right, but the words were mere sounds without any meaning. It was difficult to focus his mind on that car, on the accident. What did they matter now? He stared stupidly at the examining magistrate who was now very calm, stiff, and formal.

"It's rather remarkable, isn't it, that, up to the time of your joining the group, they had never been known to commit a misdemeanor or to do anyone any harm?"

Once again Emile turned around, this time to look uncomprehendingly at Loursat. He seemed to be floundering, to be groping for something solid to hold on to, to be asking, "What else have you been saying about me?"

"I must ask you to look at me and answer my questions. How long have you been working as shop assistant in the Librairie Georges?"

"A year."

"And before that?"

"I was at school."

"Excuse me! Weren't you employed for a while at an estate agent's in the rue Gambetta?"

The boy's eyes flashed defiance. "Yes!"

"Will you tell us under what circumstances you left?"

There was no faltering in Emile's voice as he answered. "I was dismissed. Yes, dismissed by Monsieur Goldstein himself, because there was a discrepancy of twelve francs in the petty-cash account. And he only paid me two hundred francs a month and I had to provide my own bicycle for the errands!"

"The petty cash—yes, I was coming to that. It was you who had charge of it, wasn't it? When his suspicious were aroused, he kept his eye on you for a time and finally found you were cheating on the stamps and bus fares."

A long strained silence. The rain pattered against the window. The silence outside in the corridor was more impressive still.

The prosecutor was making signs to the examining magistrate, telling him not to insist on details. But it was too late for that. Ducup persisted in his sharp voice, "What do you have to say?"

Silence.

"Then I take it you admit the theft!"

Emile Manu heaved a deep sigh. Slowly looking around him, he replied at last, "I refuse to say anything."

Finally his eyes alighted on Loursat and the expression on his face changed, as though a doubt had suddenly crossed his mind, a doubt possibly inspired by the troubled look in Loursat's large eyes.

7

HALF an hour later it was all over the Palais de Justice that Loursat was undertaking Emile Manu's defense. The lawyer was still in the prosecutor's office. The door remained closed except for a moment. Rogissart had promised his wife that he would phone her at eleven-thirty, and, not being able to make the call from his office, he went to a neighboring one.

"Why, he as good as begged the boy to allow him to take on the case!"

He was exaggerating. As a matter of fact the whole thing had been a bit of a muddle and might well have turned out otherwise.

Ducup and Rogissart were disconcerted by the young man's refusal to answer any further questions. For a minute or two they had a whispered consultation by the window. When Ducup returned to the desk, he coughed, then rather sententiously announced: "It is my duty to inform you that at this stage you have a right to obtain the assistance of a lawyer and to request his presence whenever you are being questioned."

At the mention of a lawyer, Emile had instinctively glanced at Loursat. It had really been nothing more than an association of ideas. It was all the lawyer could do not to blush. It would have been different if Emile had been older. As it was, he was little more than a child. And the feeling that gripped Loursat by the throat was itself almost childlike.

He was dying to help the boy. He felt sure that desire must be written all over his face, and he turned his head away.

Emile mistrusted him. And because he mistrusted him...

The two others, Rogissart and Ducup, had no idea what was going on. Emile's wasn't the reaction of a grown man. But Loursat understood perfectly, he wanted to understand.

Emile mistrusted him. He was saying to himself, "It may be his fault that I'm here...Though he pretends not to care, he's furious with me for compromising his daughter...Besides, isn't he related to all these people?"

And, looking at the older man, he proclaimed, "I choose Monsieur Loursat!" as if to say, "You see! I'm not afraid of you! I don't know yet whether you're my enemy or my friend, but I put myself in your hands completely and from now on you will not dare betray me!"

The prosecutor and the examining magistrate looked at each other. Ducup scratched his pointed nose with the end of his pen. As for Loursat, he answered simply, "I'll accept the case. Gentlemen, as you have pointed out yourselves, this is not an official interrogation of the prisoner. May I request that the latter should be postponed till tomorrow to give me time to study the case."

The examining magistrate sent for his clerk.

When Loursat left the room the two women jumped up from their bench. They had heard the news. Nicole looked at her father keenly. She was curious, but still on her guard. She must wait and see.

Mme Manu could hardly be expected to look at things so coolly.

They all three went down the stairs and stood in the great hall together, where people had been hanging about, hoping for a glimpse of them.

As for Loursat, he looked back at everybody with a queer expression on his face.

Mme Manu had red eyes and clutched a wadded-up handkerchief in her hand. She had not yet had time to grasp the situation and she bombarded him with questions. "Why are they keeping him, Monsieur? Surely they've no right to if they haven't charged him with anything. Where are they taking him? Can they put a person in prison before anything's proved against him? I know my boy, Monsieur Loursat, and I can assure you, if he's done anything wrong, it's the others that put him up to it."

Some of the onlookers smiled. In the legal world, the spectacle of lawyers being harassed by their clients was always considered amusing. For that reason barristers always tried to avoid such scenes in public.

Yet Loursat looked as if he was enjoying himself! Mme Manu cut rather a ridiculous figure, ridiculous and pathetic. Only, at moments, she did come near to being tragic.

"Until these last few weeks he practically never went out. Indeed I must bear some of the blame myself for what's happened. 'Emile,' I said, 'It's not healthy for a boy like you to spend evening after evening shut up all alone in your room reading. Get out. Get some fresh air. Spend time with friends your own age.' I'd have been only too happy if he'd brought them home for a chat or a game of cards."

Distraught as she was, she shot a keen glance at the lawyer from time to time, wondering how far she ought to trust him. For that matter could she trust anybody to do the right thing?

"Then he began going out with Luska, and I confess I didn't like that very much. Particularly when he started coming home later and later. Besides, he seemed to have changed. He was no longer open with me. When he went out, he never told me where he was going. Sometimes he came back so late, he couldn't have had more than three hours' sleep."

Was Loursat listening? He kept on looking at Nicole, who waited as patiently as she could, obviously anxious to get away, then back at Mme Manu, who still went on talking, occasionally dabbing her eyes.

"You'll do everything you can, won't you, Monsieur Loursat? ...Everything, no matter what it costs. I'm not well off, and with my husband's mother in the house we've never had much to spare. But at a moment like this, money doesn't count. If I have to eat dry bread for the rest of my life..."

They had been spotted by a young law student who did some writing for a Paris paper. Without taking off his robes, he dashed across the road and hurried back with a photographer who hung around outside the Palais. The photographer was carrying an enormous camera that he used for photographing weddings and school groups.

"You don't mind, do you?"

Mme Manu composed her features into a dignified expression, while Loursat stared stolidly into the camera. When it was over he said to Nicole, "You'd better take Madame Manu home. It's starting to pour. Take a taxi."

He was with them, certainly, but was he one of them? Not yet. Not quite. For he hadn't yet been *accepted*. He was conscious of that fact at lunchtime when Phine came upstairs to wait on them.

There was no need for her to do so. The new housemaid was already installed and could have done the job equally well. If Phine maintained the contrary, it was because she was anxious to hear the news and not prepared to wait till the meal was over.

She plied Nicole with questions as she went to and fro between the table and the dumbwaiter. That she did so in Loursat's presence was no mark of confidence in him. She merely ignored him.

"What did he say?"

"I don't know, Phine—I hardly saw him. He's chosen my father to defend him."

Loursat was eating—his bottle of wine nearby—as usual. He would have liked to take part in the conversation, but remained silent. Finally he came out with: "I'll see him this afternoon in the prison . . . if you have you any message for him, Nicole . . ."

"I don't think so . . . Oh yes, tell him the police searched his house but didn't find anything."

Phine was most surprised of all. And from then on kept hanging around him like a dog with a new master.

"At what time will you be seeing him?" asked Nicole.

"At three."

"Do you think . . . do you think I could come with you?"

"Not today. Tomorrow, perhaps. I'll have to ask the examining magistrate first."

They were tentative with each other, awkward.

More than any words, it was a gesture, so small that it escaped even Phine, that revealed the change in the household.

Loursat had drunk about half his bottle. Normally, at that hour, he would have already got through his first before sitting down to lunch, and then polished off the second during the meal. As he lifted the bottle to refill his glass, Nicole looked at him. He felt it, knew exactly what her glance meant. For a moment the bottle remained poised over the glass. Then he poured some wine, but no more than a mouthful, as though from modesty.

When he returned to his study a few minutes later, it occurred to him that he'd forgotten to bring up his usual bottles of wine from the cellar that morning.

The same cold rain, the prison courtyard, long corridors, a warden smoking a foul long-stemmed pipe.

"Good afternoon, Thomas."

"Good afternoon, Monsieur Loursat. It's a long time since we had the pleasure of seeing you here. It's for that boy you've come, I suppose. Where would you like to see him—in his cell or in the visitor's room? He hasn't said a word since he came here this morning and he wouldn't eat a scrap."

The sky was dull, leaden; all over town, lights were being switched on. With his briefcase tucked under his arm, Loursat followed the warden, who opened the door of no. 17, saying, "Come in, Monsieur Loursat. I'll take the other fellow away."

For Emile wasn't alone in the cell. When Loursat saw his companion, he frowned. The other man was obviously a habitué of the place, a bum they had put there to draw the boy out.

Manu was sitting in a corner. Left alone with the lawyer, he looked up but said nothing. The silence in the cell was absolute, you would never know you were in the heart of the town. What broke it was the sound of Loursat's match as he lit his cigarette.

He held out his case to the boy. "Like one?"

Emile shook his head, but the next minute he changed his mind and held out his hand. "Thanks," he said in an unsteady voice.

It was strange for the two to be alone together. Loursat felt the awkwardness particularly, and to break the spell said, "Why did you try to shoot yourself?"

"Because I didn't want to go to prison."

"Now that you're here you can see that it's not such a terrible place as people imagine. In any case, you've no reason to think you'll be here long...Who shot Big Louie?"

He was going too fast. Emile started, and it looked for a second as if he would spring to his feet.

"Why do you ask me that? You think I know, don't you? You think I did do it after all!"

"I'm convinced it wasn't you. I hope to prove it. But I'm going to find it very difficult if you don't help me."

What was so strange was not that he should find himself alone with Manu in the poorly lit cell, but that he should be questioning the young man less as a matter of professional duty than because he *wanted to know.*

It was curiosity. Not an arid, impersonal curiosity. If he could understand, it would bring him closer to this group of young people; he might even belong in some way.

It wasn't that there was anything so special about that group. It was rather what it represented: an order of things, a life within the life of the town, a particular way of feeling and thinking. It was a minuscule body revolving mysteriously in an orbit of its own.

At the same time, of course, this made them unapproachable. Particularly for a middle-aged man hunched over like a bear, with large, glaucous eyes.

"Can you tell me how you got to know these people?"

"Through Luska—I already explained it to you!"

So he was more positive than he appeared. He could remember what he had said at a time when he might easily have lost his head.

"Were they an organized band? What I mean is: did they form a sort of secret society with rules and passwords and all that sort of thing?"

Loursat threw his mind back to his own youth. He had to go much further back than Emile's age, however, to find anything comparable, for at eighteen he had already been a loner.

"There were rules."

"Written ones?"

"Yes. Edmond Dossin had a copy of them—in his wallet. He must've burned them."

"Why?"

Emile shrugged his shoulders. Perhaps he thought the question absurd. Loursat was not discouraged by his reticence. On the contrary, he had the feeling they were making progress. He held out his cigarette case again.

"I suppose it was Edmond who drew up the rules?"

"They didn't tell me, but I think so. It's his way to..."

"His way to what? To found secret societies?"

"To complicate everything. To want to have everything drawn up in documents. He made me sign a paper for Nicole."

They were getting onto very delicate ground. One misplaced word and the boy would shut up like a clam. Loursat didn't want to push. He adopted a slightly bantering tone. "What? A sort of contract?"

The boy looked down at the concrete floor. "He sold her to me... But you can't possibly understand... It was in the rules. Nobody could take another guy's girl without his consent and without paying damages."

He reddened, suddenly realizing what all this must look like to an outsider. But it was the truth.

"How much did you pay?"

"I was to pay fifty francs a month for a year."

"To Edmond? He was the previous proprietor?"

"That's what he made out, but I could see there had never been anything between them."

"I suppose my nephew will have burned that document too! He certainly seems to have been the leader of the gang."

"He was."

"Was there a name for this group?"

"The Boxing Bar Gang."

"Did Joe belong?"

"No. But of course he knew all about it. He didn't want to belong because of his license."

"I don't quite understand."

"If he had been found out, he'd have lost his license. And now that he's going straight..."

Night was falling and the light in the prison had been switched on. Now and again the regular step of a warden could be heard in the corridor.

"Did the gang meet every day?"

"In principle, yes. But Saturday was really the only day every-one had to show up, and to bring his—"

He stopped abruptly.

"His what?"

"If I tell you everything, will you be able to keep it confiden-tial?"

"I don't have the right to repeat anything you tell me with-out your express permission."

"All right. But give me another cigarette first. Mine were taken away, with everything I had on me—including my shoe-laces and—"

He was on the brink of tears. The moment before he had been talking calmly, but the sight of his laceless shoes, the feel of his collar freed of its tie, brought a sob to his throat.

"Be a man!" said Loursat without irony. "You were saying that every member had to bring something."

"Something stolen. There! I've told you. I don't want to lie. When I asked Luska to introduce me I knew that was part of the deal."

"How did you know?"

"I'd been told."

"By who?"

"It could've been almost any kid in town . . . They didn't know all the details, of course, but there was talk about the gang."

"Did you have to swear allegiance?"

"I had to sign a paper."

"Were you put through a test?"

"That was the car. If I hadn't known how to drive I would've had to break into an empty house, stay there for an hour, and bring back a trophy."

"It didn't matter what it was?"

"No. But the bigger and heavier they were, the better it was. It was a sort of contest. Luska turned up once with a twenty-pound pumpkin."

"And what did you do with all these things?"

No answer from Emile.

"Am I right in assuming they're in my house?"

"In the attic, yes."

"Had this been going on a long time—I mean before you joined them?"

"About two months. Perhaps not quite. I think Edmond picked up the idea at Aix-les-Bains, where he spent the holidays. Kids there did the same thing."

But when had Nicole become so close to her cousin? The answer had come to him vaguely two or three days ago, when he was holed up in his den. But it was only now that he remembered that his sister Marthe had written to tell him they were taking a house at Aix-les-Bains for the summer and to invite Nicole to join them there.

She had stayed a whole month. But, as he had never taken any interest in her doings, the fact had hardly sunk in.

So this is what the well-to-do young people who vacationed in Aix-les-Bains got up to while their parents were frequenting spas and casinos!

"Did Edmond bring things in, like the others?"

"Once he brought a silver-plated coffeepot belonging to the Brasserie Gambetta. But another time there was an argument because Destrivaux accused him of being too afraid to do the real thing and of passing off things from his own house as stolen goods. When Big Louie let it slip that he had a police record, you should have heard Edmond brag about our crimes."

"And this took place in the room on the third floor?"

"Yes. He wanted to show off! It was the worst thing he could do. It only encouraged Big Louie to blackmail us. He said he was out of work because of us and had to have some money to send to his wife. He said he wanted a thousand francs a day."

"You all got together to raise it?"

"No. The others left it all to me."

"You had to find all that money?"

"Yes."

He wasn't crying, but he turned his face to the wall anyway. Then he felt the need to look Loursat in the eye. "What could I do? Everyone was saying it was my fault, that I shouldn't have pretended I knew how to drive...But because of Big Louie, I was able to go and see Nicole every evening...I have to tell you everything, don't I? You're my lawyer...You wanted to do it...I don't know why, but you wanted to...Well, you've made your own bed...If only I could have run away with Nicole, anywhere..."

"What did she say?"

"Nothing."

"Where did you find the thousand francs?"

"At home. My mother doesn't know yet. I went to the place where she keeps her savings—in her underwear drawer, in an old wallet that belonged to my father."

"What about the other money?"

"What other money?"

"The other sixteen hundred francs?"

"Who told you about it?"

"Unfortunately, it's in the prosecutor's file. The police traced the money orders sent in Big Louie's name."

"What is there to prove I sent them?"

"Nothing. But they suspect you all the same."

"Luska lent me four hundred francs. As for the rest, I suppose I'd better tell you since it's bound to come out sooner or later. I was at my wit's end. Big Louie was threatening every day to get in touch with the police...Do you know Monsieur Testut?"

"What, that old man who lives in the place d'Armes?"

"Yes. He's a customer...buys lots of books, including expensive ones that we have to get specially for him from Paris. He came into the shop one day when Monsieur Georges was upstairs having his tea. The old man always goes up at four o'clock for a cup of tea. Monsieur Testut came to pay his bill— one thousand three hundred and thirty-two francs—I kept the money. I meant to pay it back at the end of the month."

"How?"

"Somehow...I'd have found a way. I swear I'm not a thief. Besides, I told Edmond..."

"Told him what?"

"That I wasn't going to be the scapegoat for them all. That they'd have to help me...that if they hadn't gotten me drunk on the night of the accident—"

The sound of a car horn in the distance penetrated the thick layers of silence around them, reminding them that they were in the middle of a town, a little town whose inhabitants thought they knew everything that went on around them.

Why was Loursat reminded at just that moment of the Club de Palais? It had no conceivable connection with the subject they were discussing.

A few years before, at the time when contract bridge was just coming into fashion, a group of magistrates and lawyers decided it was time for Moulins to have a club. A letter was sent around to all the leading personalities in town. An organizing committee was formed, with Ducup as its secretary.

Premises were procured at the corner of the avenue Victor-Hugo. And at a general meeting a permanent executive committee was elected with Rogissart as president and a general —no club would be complete without a general—as vice-president.

Loursat found that his name had been put on the list of members. Not because he was involved, but because of his position. He even received their expensively printed newsletter.

But even though he held resolutely aloof, he couldn't help hearing something of the new membership controversy. On one side were those who insisted that the club remain select, and on the other were those who took a more democratic view. For instance, three meetings were devoted to the case of a doctor whom some wanted to let in, but who was barred by the others because he specialized in cosmetic surgery.

In the course of a more than usually stormy meeting, Ducup, who was still secretary, had joined Rogissart in resigning from the club and a good half of the members had followed their lead.

People talked of nothing else for weeks, until the day that several tradesmen had demanded payment, and it was discovered that the club manager had been approving some odd expenditures. To keep the matter from going to court, each member, including those who had resigned, was asked to cough up some money. Not everyone had gone along with the plan.

"Tell me, Manu..."

He had been about to call him Emile.

"I must know the names of all the members of your gang, as you call it. Another thing—did Big Louie ever speak of a friend of his coming to see him?"

"No."

"Or of his mistress coming to Moulins?"

"No."

"There was never any talk in the gang of getting rid of him, was there?"

"Yes."

At that moment the warden knocked on the door and poked his head in.

"Here's a letter for you, Maître Loursat. It's from the prosecutor's office by messenger."

Loursat tore open the envelope and found a typewritten note.

The public prosecutor has the honor of informing Maître Loursat that Jean Destrivaux has been reported missing by his parents. He has not been seen since yesterday evening.

The situation was getting more and more confused. And for eighteen years Loursat had forgotten the people around him.

Yet he had a tantalizing feeling that if he just tried a little harder, everything would begin to fit into place.

"Destrivaux..." he began in a strained voice.

"Yes?"

"What do you think about him?"

"He's a neighbor. His parents built a house on our street."

"How did he fit into the gang?"

"It's difficult to explain, especially to anyone who's never seen him. A pale, silent fellow with glasses. Thought he was smarter than everybody else. More objective, he called it."

"He's disappeared. That's what this note's about."

Emile was thoughtful, his face a curious mixture of childish despair and keen concentration.

"No," he said at last.

"No what?"

"I can't believe he did it—stealing lighters was his thing."

The effort it took to follow the boy's train of thought was beginning to exhaust Loursat. He had to decipher every phrase, like a code-breaker. "I don't understand," he confessed.

"They're the easiest things to steal...He used to buy his cigarettes from tobacconists who had a display of lighters on the counter. He'd manage to knock some over with his sleeve, then pick them up all apologies, slipping one into his pocket."

"Look here, Manu—"

Once again, he almost said Emile. The question he was going to ask was, "What was the motive for that kind of theft?"

But no. It was silly. Anyone would understand. Instead, he said, "All the same, it was one of you who—"

"Yes, it was one of us..."

"Who?"

A silence. Emile stared at the floor. Then: "I don't know."

"Edmond?"

"I don't think so. Unless, of course..."

"Unless what?"

"Unless he was afraid."

For the first time that day Loursat missed his burgundy. He was tired, sagging.

"You'll probably be taken to the Palais de Justice for questioning at nine o'clock tomorrow morning. I'll try to see you beforehand. In any case I'll be there. The important thing is not to answer too quickly. Take your time. And if you're in doubt about anything, ask my advice openly. I think you'll have to tell them about the thefts."

He noticed that Emile looked disappointed. Loursat was feeling the same, though he couldn't have said why. Perhaps he had hoped to make an immediate and intimate contact with the young man and was discouraged by the invisible barriers between them.

As for Emile, what help had he been given? He had been advised to think before he spoke, but that was about all. Otherwise, he was left drifting.

Almost immediately the door opened again and Loursat reappeared. "I'd forgotten. I'll take immediate steps to have your cell mate changed. This one's a plant. And be on your guard against anyone they replace him with."

It was true that there was thirty years' difference in their ages. How could they be expected to click all at once?

With his briefcase in his left hand, Loursat halted in the prison entrance. He looked at the street lamps and their reflections on the glistening pavements, then caught sight of a small café a little way down the street on the right-hand side. He hurried toward it and pushed open the door.

"A glass of red wine, please."

It was none too soon. Inwardly he was sinking rapidly, regretting having ever left his sanctuary and his solitude.

The proprietor, in a pullover with rolled-up sleeves, watched the lawyer gulp down the wine, then asked, "It'll stir up quite a lot of mud, won't it? They say some of the best families are shaking in their boots."

So it was already all over town!

"Another, please."

It was a dark-colored wine, rough and heavy.

Loursat paid and hurried off again. He had been out and about in the company of men for too long, for his first sortie. Does a convalescent walk from dawn till dusk the first day he's allowed out?

All the same, he was almost tempted to make a little detour so as to pass by the Palais de Justice.

Just to sniff around the enemy's camp!

PART TWO

8

LOURSAT threw a sidelong glance at his daughter, then went over to poke the fire in the stove, which crackled loudly with every gust of wind on that wild night. Nicole, he knew, was conscious of all his movements, though her eyes never left the pages of the files over which she was bending attentively. Even so, he sidled up to the cupboard, from which he took a bottle of rum.

"You're not feeling cold?" he asked awkwardly.

She answered no in a tone that mingled a hint of reproach with indulgence. There had been many nights he'd returned the bottle to the shelf without taking a drink. This time he helped himself, though with the murmured excuse:

"It's our last night... Tomorrow..."

It was already after midnight. The sky was cold and clear, the streets were swept clean by the boisterous wind that whipped up the fine particles of ice from the sidewalks.

Neither of them had thought of closing the shutters, and the light from the lawyer's study shone out into the street, the one patch of light among the darkened houses.

They had reached the end of the tunnel, a tunnel that was three months long. On the first day of January the wet pall of cloud that had hung so long over Moulins had lifted, enabling people to go about their business without hugging the walls and trying to dodge the drips, in a world that was eternally black and white, smudged like a bad charcoal drawing.

The nights had been so long that people scarcely recalled the days. Looking back one remembered only badly lit shops, misty windows, shadow-filled streets where each passerby became mysterious.

"How far have you got?" asked Loursat, sitting down again and lighting a cigarette.

"I've done sixty-three."

"You're not sleepy?"

She shook her head. Sixty-three folders out of ninety-seven. Ninety-seven folders of yellow paper that lay in piles on the desk. Some were bulky, some flat. Some contained no more than a single document.

In the middle of the mantelpiece, starkly black on white, was a huge figure, 12. Sunday, January 12. That page of the calendar should already have been torn off to give place to that of Monday, January 13. In other words, today was the day.

Perhaps for others it meant nothing, but for Loursat, for Nicole, for Phine, for the maid, and for others too in greater or less degree, this was the end of the tunnel. By eight o'clock special guards would be on duty on the steps of the Palais de Justice to make sure that no one entered the building except the few who had been granted passes. A prison van would drive up at a side door and out of it would step Emile, thinner now but taller, who would be wearing a new suit that his mother had made the week before. Still later Loursat would put on the robes which Nicole had taken to the cleaners.

"Pijollet?" she asked suddenly, frowning, "wasn't he questioned twice?"

Who cared who this Pijollet was? They did. They and a handful of others who were by now so immersed in the case that they could communicate in their own secret language.

"No. Only once," he answered promptly. "On the twelfth of December."

"I've got that one . . . but I thought there was a second."

Pijollet was a neighbor of Destrivaux, and of Manu too, since he lived on the same street. An elderly man, he had formerly been second or third violin at the Paris Opera, returning to live in his native town on his retirement.

"No. I don't know the Manus, though I knew that a lady on the block gave piano lessons...As for the Destrivaux, I could often see them sitting in their garden...in summer, of course...The walls are thin and when they sat down to eat I could hear their voices...not clearly enough to make out what they were saying ...What I could hear was the sound of the front door every time it was opened or shut...I never go to sleep before two in the morning...a legacy of my work, no doubt...I read in bed...And I couldn't fail to notice that one of the people next door—I took it to be the young Jean Destrivaux—often came home very late... Sometimes I'd even gone to sleep and was woken up with a start."

All that rigmarole just to lead up to Ducup's question:

"Can you remember the night of the seventh to eighth of October?"

"Clearly."

"What makes you so positive?"

"The fact that on the afternoon of the eighth, I met a friend whom I believed to be still in Madagascar."

"But what makes you remember the date?"

"We went into a café to have a chat. It's a very rare thing for me to set foot in a café. And right in front of me, where I was sitting, was a calendar...Looking back I can clearly see the figure seven... I distinctly remember hearing the Destrivaux's front door shut at two o'clock in the morning, just as I was settling down to sleep."

Ninety-seven folders, one for each person who figured in the case, many of whom had stepped out of their anonymity to become, for the moment at least, important people—a policeman on duty, a café waitress, a girl at one of the counters of Prisunic, a customer of the Librairie Georges, each one made their contribution to the gigantic dossier, which Nicole was now putting in order for the last time.

At eight o'clock that morning the court would inaugurate a fresh session with the indictment of Emile Manu for the murder of Louis Gagalin, otherwise known as Big Louie, at about twenty minutes to twelve on the night of the eighth day of October in the house of Hector Dominique François Loursat de Saint-Marc.

Three months of gray skies and almost incessant rain, and this was the result—a dossier of ninety-seven manila folders on each of which a name was neatly written in violet ink.

But day by day, hour by hour, each folder, each page came to life, became a man or a woman, with a job, a house, and their own faults, vices, interests, ways of talking or behaving.

So many people—at first there had been no more than a handful: Edmond Dossin, whose parents had sent him to a clinic in Switzerland; the beefy Daillat of the charcuterie; Jean Destrivaux, who had been picked up in Paris wandering hungrily about a vegetable market without so much as a franc in his pocket; Luska on the pavement outside Prisunic now selling a cheap line of heavy hunting boots.

Then a young man called Grouin, who hadn't spent much time with the Boxing Bar Gang, but who was nonetheless a member even if he had dropped out. His father was a *conseiller général*.

Every morning for the past three months—excluding for the last few weeks—Emile Manu had left the prison with a gendarme on either side on the way to the Palais de Justice. Indeed his day's employment was just about as regular and monotonous as it had been at the Librairie Georges.

Even if Ducup knew perfectly well he wouldn't need the prisoner till eleven o'clock, he insisted on his being at his disposal from eight o'clock onward. When Emile arrived at the Palais the lights were still burning in the corridors and women were scrubbing the floors. He was put into a small squalid room: dirty walls, a bench, and, in a corner, two mop buckets. For furniture, there was merely a wooden bench, on which he and one of the gendarmes would sit down while the other went off for a cup of coffee. When he returned twenty minutes later a smell of rum would be hanging about his moustache... Then the other would go.

The electric light paled as the daylight invaded the room. Before long steps could be heard overhead. That would be Ducup arriving, taking his place at his desk, calling in his clerk, and summoning the first of the day's crop of witnesses.

Doubtless there were people in the town who had other matters to bother about, but for quite a number the whole world pivoted about the events that had occurred on the night of the seventh to eighth of October.

"Is your name Sophie Stüff and are you the owner of an inn at Les Coqueteaux?"

"Yes, Your Honor."

"You were born in Strasburg, where your husband, Stüff, was a street sweeper?... Left a widow with two daughters, Eva and Clara, you settled in Brettignies where you earned your living as daily help... You were the mistress of a certain Troulet, against whom you once lodged a complaint for assault."

That was the woman who kept the Auberge aux Noyés. Her evidence, together with that of her daughters, took up five pages. Not content with that, Loursat had returned three or four times to the place, to sit meditatively as he stared at the framed photograph of Stüff, who stared back with a startled expression on his face. There were other photographs too—of Eva and Clara as little girls, of a man in a gendarme's uniform who turned out to be Troulet, the one who used to beat her.

"When the so-called gang came to your place, who appeared to be its leader?... Who paid, for instance?"

"Monsieur Edmond always paid."

He did indeed. Only Loursat had learned from Nicole that before setting out for the place the others had each had to contribute their share.

"When he danced he pulled his cap over to one side and let his cigarette dangle from his lip ... He brought records along, because we didn't have any. It was music they played in the dance halls, he said ..."

"Did he ever make advances to you?"

This was during Eva's evidence.

"No. He carried on as though we were beneath him. He used to call us sluts and pretended to think that we ... in the house ..."

"Go on, tell us."

"Don't you get it? He thought that there were rooms upstairs, that we'd go up there with anyone, he wouldn't stop talking about it."

"Did he ever ask you to go up with him?"

"No ... But the red-faced fellow—Monsieur Daillat, I mean—he was worse."

"What did he do?"

"He could never keep his hands to himself. You'd push him off and he'd start up again the next minute ... If it wasn't me it was my sister, and he'd have tried it with my mother if she'd given him the chance ... He didn't care who it was so long as it was in a skirt, and he was always telling filthy stories ..."

Ducup and Loursat no longer shook hands. When Loursat went to the magistrate's office for a deposition, Ducup would say coldly, "Excuse me ... Would you be so kind ... If the counsel for the defense would be so good as to ..."

And Loursat seemed to bring to the Palais—together with his scrubby beard, his baggy clothes, and the grease spots on his vest—strange echoes of another world into which he plunged after dark, to return with yet another person whose existence had hitherto been unsuspected, another name to be neatly inscribed on another manila folder.

It was he who had discovered M. Pijollet. It was he who had

dragged, almost by the scruff of his neck, the corpulent M. Luska, Ephraïm Luska, whose thighs were so fat he could only waddle.

Terrified by the examining magistrate, the shopkeeper had stammered, "I thought my boy must be in love. I said so to his mother. We were both very concerned about him."

Inspector Binet too went hunting in the back alleys of the town, sometimes producing a new witness.

Almost all the manila folders now lay stacked in a single pile. The stove roared fitfully. And Nicole held herself very erect in her chair so as not to show that she was falling asleep.

It was she who had been acting as secretary, taking down notes, copying documents, and promptly producing any particular paper that was wanted. One day Loursat made the mistake of speaking to her in the familiar form.

He had worked long into the night, when they were the only two people awake in the house, in the street, perhaps in the whole town, and Loursat would gaze longingly at his liquor cabinet. He never brought more than one bottle of burgundy up from the cellar nowadays, and he drank it sparingly. Admittedly he'd discovered a little bar tucked away behind the Palais de Justice where they served a rather good Beaujolais. At first he'd made it a strict rule to have one glass only. Then one day he had slipped, and thenceforward the proprietor filled his glass a second time without waiting to be asked.

But he didn't get drunk now. Never! On the contrary, he would say that he rarely filled his quota these days, and needed, as he did now, a few mouthfuls of rum to bring him up to scratch.

"I'm underlining a contradiction in Bergot's testimony," Nicole said, marking it in red. "He says it was on the twenty-first of October that Emile came to him to sell his watch. But according to his dossier it would have been the fourteenth or fifteenth. Bergot is off by a week at least."

Bergot! There was another whose existence no one had suspected. A watchmaker, whose shopfront, jammed in between a butcher's and a grocer's on the other side of the market, was so narrow that you could pass it every day for months without noticing it.

Bergot was a huge gelatinous creature with a pendulous stomach and a rancid smell. In the examining magistrate's room he had the appearance of someone who hadn't left his lair—where he lived surrounded by old broken-down watches and old-fashioned jewelry that no one would think of wearing nowadays—in years.

Yet he came suddenly to life! So did all the others. And when you spoke one of their names, it didn't sound like an ordinary name.

It was the mention of Bergot's name that suddenly made Loursat realize what he felt like—he was like a scholar who has devoted years to a monumental work, a ten-volume study of coleoptera, or a book about the Fourth Dynasty.

There they were, on the table, each folder stuffed with words that were for most people insignificant.

Bergot . . . Pijollet . . . Mme Stüff . . .

To him, though, each name was replete with meaning, with life, with drama. The pile of folders stood like a great column, and yet . . .

He got up and, in spite of Nicole's presence, went over to the cabinet again, though this time he only took half a glass of rum.

Now that the work was over the main thing was not to lose heart. In coming out of the tunnel, he must not let himself slip back into his old existence.

What had existed was Big Louie. Big Louie dead, of course —alive he held no interest.

And someone had killed him.

Then again, there was someone who hadn't killed him: Emile, who for the last three months had alternated between dejection and almost hysterical outbursts of passion. More than once he had been dragged out of the examining magistrate's room shouting at the top of his voice, "I tell you I'm innocent. You've no right to try and pin it on me. You're a filthy brute."

Yes, he had called Ducup a filthy brute. At other moments he had been as meek as a lamb, asking, "Will there be a lot of people there? Is it true the Paris papers are sending reporters?"

Having wound up his end of the case, Ducup, exhausted, took advantage of the Christmas holidays to get a breath of mountain air. The whole thing had become stifling; it gave you the feeling that you weren't surrounded by living people, but by shadows.

On three occasions since that fatal night, the butcher Daillat and his son had come to blows, and even kicks.

"You needn't think I'm afraid of you," shouted the young man.

"You're nothing but a dirty thief."

"I wouldn't have learned it from you by any chance, would I?"

And bystanders would have to separate them. Once the police were called in to find the boy's face covered with blood.

As for Destrivaux, when he had been found in Paris he had stoutly refused to return to Moulins. He couldn't face people, he said. His father went to the capital and together they decided that the best thing the boy could do was to go straight into the army without waiting to be called up for military service.

He was in the paymaster's office at Orléans in a uniform that was much too large for him, wearing his glasses, of course, his face covered with pimples.

He had had four sessions with Ducup, and on one of them, Manu confronted him.

"I can't understand how I brought myself to do it . . . I let myself be pushed into it by the others . . . No. I never stole any money, not even from my parents."

They had managed to keep news of the thefts under wraps. The elder Dossin paid everybody off, the shopkeepers were happy to keep their mouths shut, and the local paper was discreet.

Even so, there were some in town who knew about the whole affair. It was almost as if there were two towns: the familiar town, which seemed devoid of meaning and substance, and the town that revolved around the case, full of dark corners and unexpected characters conjured up by Loursat from words on paper.

"You won't be too tired for the trial?"

Nicole smiled almost reproachfully. Had she ever wavered, ever lost faith? Throughout, she had remained exactly as she had always been, quiet, composed, serene. Where haggard looks would have seemed quite proper, she was almost indecently round, plump, and healthy.

She hadn't lost an ounce. Yet she hadn't taken so much as an afternoon off since she settled down to her task. Every day on his return from the Palais, her father would find her in his study, cool, businesslike, and sweet-tempered.

She picked up the last folder, which contained a single sheet of the type of cheap writing paper sold in grocers' shops. The writing was that of an uneducated woman. The pen was the sort you find in a café or a post office; its rough nib had scratched and sputtered along the paper.

Monsieur,

You're right to think Manu innocent. Don't worry about him. If he's condemned, I'll come forward myself and say who killed Big Louie. I know.

It had come by post the day after Christmas, and so far all efforts to find the writer had been in vain, though Loursat had enlisted the help of the police.

At first he had thought it might be Angèle, the former

housemaid whom he had paid off—there was a time Loursat had even suspected her of being Big Louie's killer.

He'd gone to Nevers, where she now worked as a waitress in a café, to collect a writing sample from her.

No. It wasn't Angèle.

Big Louie's mistress, the one he had been sending money to in Honfleur, was another possibility. Again he had drawn a blank.

Inquiries had been made in the two brothels in town, since it is often to prostitutes that criminals unburden themselves when they can no longer bottle up their secret.

Ducup, on the other hand, maintained it was a hoax, though he obviously suspected its being a doubtful maneuver on the part of the defense.

They had waited for a follow-up—people who write anonymous letters of that sort are rarely content with one.

And now at ten minutes to one on the morning of January 13 Loursat and Nicole suddenly started and looked at each other in surprise. The front-door bell had been given such a tug that a veritable peal sounded in the hall.

Overhead, they could hear Phine turn over in bed, but there was no danger of her coming down to answer it.

Loursat was already on his way to the door. He went down the stairs and across the hall, feeling for the bolt.

A familiar voice said, "I saw your light was still on."

It was Joe, the retired boxer, who came in, muttering, "Can I have a word with you?"

Although Loursat had spent many an evening at the Boxing Bar, Joe had never set foot in the house, and he looked around him with curiosity. In the study, he nodded to Nicole, then hesitated, not knowing whether he ought to sit down or stand.

"I think I've just done something stupid," he began, half-sitting on a corner of the desk. "You'll probably curse me for a fool, and you'll be quite right to."

He took a cigarette from the packet Loursat held out, glanced at the pile of folders.

"You know what it's like at my place. Some nights you can't hear yourself speak...Today, though, there were just four of us. You know Adèle, Adèle Pigasse to give her her full name, the one who squints and whose beat is on the corner...She's got a man, Gène from Bordeaux—he wrestles at the fair. He was there too...Then there was La Gourde, the fat girl who specializes in soldiers...Well we were sitting there quietly, playing belote, to pass the time away till bedtime...And then, I don't really know why, I suddenly said: " 'The lawyer's been nice to me. He's given me a pass.'

"You see, we always call you the lawyer...Then Adèle asked was it a pass for the trial, and when I said yes she asked if I couldn't get one for her. I told her they were very hard to come by because everybody wanted to be there, and she got mad.

" 'Just like you to forget your pals,' she said.

" 'If you wanted a pass why didn't you ask him yourself?'

" 'I've got more right to one than you have!'

" 'I'd like to know why.'

" 'Never mind why!'

"We kept on playing. Then I said again, 'I can't see you getting up at eight in the morning, anyway!'

" 'Then you might've been surprised!'

" 'Oh, come on,' said Gène. 'Drop it. Let's get on with the game.'

" 'Anyhow,' said Adèle. 'I could get a pass quicker than anybody else if I wanted to.'

" 'How?'

" 'And I would sit in the very front row too!'

" 'Yeah, right, you'd be right next to the judges!'

" 'No. With the witnesses.'

" 'Well, in the first place the witnesses aren't in the front row, they're kept behind the scenes. In the second place you're not a witness.'

" 'Only because I don't want to be,' she said.

" 'Because you don't know anything about it.'

" 'All right. Have it your way. Whose turn is it?'

"We started the game up again. Gène looked at her odd-like, because Adèle doesn't carry on like that. We finish the game and I stand the last round of drinks. Then if Adèle didn't lift her glass and say, 'To the murderer!'

" 'I suppose you know who he is?'

" 'Suppose I do.'

" 'What do you mean?'

"Then La Gourde chimed in to say, 'Can't you see she's trying to make herself look interesting?'

"But I knew it wasn't that. I could see Adèle had something on her mind, and I was set on getting it out of her. And I knew the best way was to pretend I didn't believe her. The next minute she was blabbing, 'I do too know who did it. What's more, I know where he stashed the gun.'

" 'Where's that?'

" 'I'm not telling . . . One night when he was just about at the end of his tether . . .'

" 'So you went to bed with him, did you?'

" 'Three times.'

" 'Who is it?'

" 'I won't say.'

" 'But you'll tell me, won't you?' said Gène.

" 'Not you or anybody else,' she answered.

"I thought it was about time to get tough with her. I told her that was no way to treat me, not with all the money she owed me and all the times I'd given her sandwiches when she didn't have a penny . . .

" 'If you don't tell me . . .' I said, going right up to her.

" 'Never!'

"With that I gave her a slap right in the face and told her that she disgusted me, called her a dirty little bitch.

"I really was wild with her and I let her have it. I don't know what I didn't say to her... In the end I chucked her out, and Gène too, as he began to take sides with her, which was a bit thick considering all the things I've got on him... But there! We don't need to go into that...

"When they'd gone, La Gourde and I looked at each other, and I wondered whether I'd done right, seeing as how I got nothing much out of Adèle after all... Then I thought, since the trial's tomorrow, you might still be up..."

"Do you know her handwriting?" asked Loursat, opening the last of the folders.

"I don't even know if she can hold a pen... Oh, yes, I do... Twice she's written letters to her boy from my place. She's got a five-year-old in a sanatorium somewhere or other. But I didn't see the letters themselves."

"Where does she live?"

"Near me... There's an old woman called La Morue who has some rooms at the back of a courtyard and lets them by the week."

Loursat had just enough time to sneak once more to his cabinet for another mouthful of rum. Fifteen minutes later he was following Joe down a narrow alley that led into a cobbled courtyard littered with garbage cans and packing cases and surrounded by the peeling walls of ancient houses, between which stretched wire clotheslines hung with washing.

Joe knocked on a door. Sounds within. Finally a sleepy voice queried, "Who is it?"

"It's me... Joe... Can I speak to Adèle?... It's important..."

"She's not here."

"She's not back yet?"

"She came in but then went off again."

"With Gène?"

"I don't know whether she was with anybody."

A window opened above and a head emerged. By the light of the moon they could see it was La Gourde.

"I think Gène was waiting for her outside... You know, Joe, you really scared her."

"I want to have a word with her," Loursat whispered to Joe.

"Look here," said the latter, "can we come up for a moment?"

"The room's a mess..."

They climbed the unlit circular staircase. La Gourde came out of her room in a gaudy dressing gown carrying an oil lamp. "I'm sorry for the mess, Monsieur Loursat, but I've had company twice this evening..."

She had pushed the enamel bidet behind the bed.

"Do you mind if I get back into bed? It's freezing."

"There's something I want to ask you... You work in much the same area as Adèle, don't you?... Can you tell me which young people in this town have had anything to do with her?"

"Before or after?"

Unthinkingly, he asked, "After what?"

"After Big Louie... After all the trouble began... Yes, before. I remember there was Monsieur Edmond Dossin... It was his first time. He wanted to see what it was like... But he had a few problems, if you know what I mean..."

"And after?"

"I really don't know. She told me all about it because he was really angry and had given her a hundred francs not to tell anyone."

"You haven't seen her with any of them?"

"Wait a minute... I'm thinking... No, I haven't really. To tell the truth I don't usually get a glimpse of them. They mostly try not to be seen."

"You don't know where she went?"

"She didn't say where she was going...All I know is that she has a married sister in Paris who lives somewhere near the Observatory. She's a concierge...She's also got a brother. I think he's in the mounted police, but I've no idea where."

Ducup awoke with a start at the sound of his telephone ringing. After that it was Inspector Binet's turn. A few minutes later a handful of men left the police station, some on bicycles, some on foot. At three o'clock Binet left his home to supervise operations from headquarters.

Every hotel in the town was searched, and there were police officers waiting at the bus and train stations by the time rush hour began.

At eight o'clock in the morning the doors to the Palais de Justice were opened. Outside, behind barriers, a crowd of some two hundred people thronged eagerly beneath the icy sky.

9

IT SHOULDN'T have been a surprise, yet Loursat couldn't help frowning: Mme Manu was there, in the little room where her son was waiting between two gendarmes.

Oddly, the scene called to mind a marriage or a first communion. The people—red-nosed, hands stuffed into pockets or holding passes aloft—converging just as the church bell rang; the robed lawyers moving with a priestly sense of the importance of their gestures; and Manu, who—dressed in his new navy-blue suit and his squeaky new patent leather shoes—was pronounced very handsome by his mother. Hadn't she just been adjusting his tie?

Madame was in her best black clothes and wearing just the merest hint of perfume. She was weeping without tears. It had become a habit with her. She rushed up to the lawyer, and for a moment he feared she would bury her face in his bosom.

"I put my son in your hands, Monsieur Loursat. He is all I have left in the world."

Of course! Of course! Yet he had the feeling that if the case went on much longer—if there was an appeal—he'd finish by hating her with all his might. She was too good! And everything she said was invariably the proper thing. She was too dignified, modest, she showed all the feelings which a woman should show in her position.

How could anyone help pitying her? A poor widow who had slaved for years to keep her only son at school, who had held nothing but good examples up before his eyes, only to see him end up in court.

She ought to have been a tragic figure, yet if the truth was told, she rarely was. Only at those moments when she forgot her dignity and upbringing and gazed around her with the panic-stricken eyes of a child lost in the street did she approach tragedy.

He didn't like her. There it was! Moreover he couldn't help feeling sure that Emile had been stifled by all the motherly care he got in their spotlessly clean house in the rue Ernest-Voivenon.

"You still hold out hope, don't you, Monsieur Loursat?"

"I certainly do, Madame!"

There was the usual last-minute scramble, the usual anxiety as to what might have been forgotten. The president of the court, already in his red robes, kept peering around the door, wondering whether the place was going to be warm enough. The windowpanes were frosted over, the streetlights glittered with ice.

Loursat glanced into the witnesses' room and saw Nicole sitting demurely at the end of the bench.

The police had not yet been able to find Adèle Pigasse or Gène from Bordeaux. Ducup looked ghastly, his eyes red-rimmed, for his health was not too good, and after Loursat's telephone call he had been unable to fall back to sleep.

"Gentlemen, the Court!"

Loursat rushed, sleeves flowing, toward his bench with such a forbidding expression on his face that no one would have been surprised to hear him growl.

He placed the ninety-seven manila folders in front of him with a look of defiance aimed toward the public, then at the judges. His every hair bristled.

The jury was chosen by lot.

"Does the defense wish to raise any objection?"

"No objection."

Joe was there, right in the front row, looking as though he

was a member of the family. The clerk of the court proceeded to muster the witnesses while the public talked excitedly.

"This is a very delicate case," the president announced sadly. "I must warn the public that I will tolerate no outbursts whatsoever. At the first sign of disorder I will promptly clear the court."

M. Niquet, that was his name. He had frequented the Loursats' house in Hector's father's time. A kind man, indeed oozing with kindness. His angelic blue eyes not only proclaimed the fact but seemed to be beseeching the world to think no less kindly of him.

Unfortunately the expression was marred by his mouth and chin. His chin was as broad as the rest of his face and quite flat, while the mouth, which was always slightly slack, went from ear to ear. It was a real blemish, for it gave him a silly sarcastic grin that completely belied the almost melancholy pensiveness which his intimates knew him to possess.

"I must explain to the jury that the prosecution has refrained from calling one of the principal witnesses, Monsieur Hector Loursat de Saint-Marc, in order that he might undertake the accused man's defense. I can assure the jury, however, that his absence from the witness box cannot affect the case one way or the other, since the facts to which he would testify are not in dispute."

Everybody looked curiously at the lawyer, while he, like a wild beast in a cage, slowly turned his head and returned their stare.

As for Emile, sitting between his two guards, dressed in dark blue, that white bow-tie, he really did look just like a boy going up for his first communion; or, at any rate, extremely young. He gazed fixedly at the floor, but after a while, having summoned up his courage, he looked anxiously at the many familiar faces in the crowd.

In spite of the crowd, the courtroom was bitterly cold, and

the president interrupted proceedings for a moment to promise the jury he would try to have some heating arranged. After all, they would probably have to sit there for three whole days.

The indictment. Then Emile was asked to plead.

"Not guilty," he answered quietly, looking steadily at Loursat.

Then it was the lawyer's turn to get to his feet. "Monsieur le Président, a recently discovered fact obliges me to ask the court to postpone the case until some future date. Last night a woman was heard to state that she knew who had killed Louis Gagalin."

"Where is this woman?"

"The police are looking for her, meanwhile..."

There was a long huddle. The judges called Rogissart, who in turn called Ducup. Finally the president said, "I am assured that the police will continue to make every effort to find this Adèle Pigasse and that as soon as she is found she will be brought here. In the meantime there is no reason why the court shouldn't proceed with the hearing of the other witnesses."

It was Ducup who, for an hour and a quarter, gave a detailed report of his interrogations.

"...eighteen years of age...already distinguished himself by petty theft from his first employers...lonely and suspicious...Until the day he joined the group at the Boxing Bar, it had not attracted any attention...He became intoxicated... vanity that caused him to steal the car of a respected citizen... Manu is proud, insatiable. What interests him is less to enjoy himself as others of his age do, than to break into—and by the service entrance!—into the house of one of the finest families, a family that represents..."

His words cut like a knife. Now and again he glanced at Loursat with a sneer.

"His responses, his attitude, are inspired by the same pride, the same desire to assert himself...His fake suicide attempt during his arrest has been but one more attempt to make himself appear interesting."

Loursat couldn't help looking at Emile, and a vague smile flitted across his face.

All that the examining magistrate was saying about the boy's character was perfectly true! The lawyer had known all along that Emile was eaten up by a sense of his own inferiority.

Once he had been to see Emile's mother in her house in the rue Ernest-Voivenon. The next day Emile had asked him with a bitter smile, "I suppose she showed you the watercolors? The house is full of them. They were my father's hobby, he used to spend all his evenings and Sundays copying postcards!"

A little later on he had come back to the subject: "In my room there's a washstand, with a bowl and a jug decorated with roses. Only, I'm not allowed to use it, because it's very fragile. I have to make do with an enamel basin on a wooden table, with a strip of linoleum underneath."

He suffered from it all: from his ugly-colored cheap raincoat, the shoes that had been resoled several times, the respectful way in which his mother would refer to the rich and the way they lived.

It was embarrassing to be seen dusting the shelves of the Librairie Georges, to wait on his old schoolmates. Gazing out of the shop window he could see young men like Edmond Dossin and his fellow students at the Ecole des Hautes Etudes who, laughing and talking, would saunter up and down the rue d'Allier before going home for lunch.

For him there were the errands to do, carrying heavy parcels and as often as not being given a tip by the servant who opened the door.

Those were things Ducup would never know, but he had nonetheless hit the nail on the head.

"... suspicious ... stubborn ..."

That was painful enough, but Ducup continued:

"Yet, at home, he has had nothing but good examples before his eyes."

Loursat glanced again at the boy. The best examples in the world, for God's sake! You had only to take one look at his father's photograph to see that: his gaze gentle and contented despite the tubercular flush and painfully thin shoulders.

The elder Manu had been an industrial designer specializing in agricultural machinery at the Dossin factory—was head of technical services, in fact. He'd come from Capestang, where his mother still lived. After his death, his wife had gone on sending the her two hundred francs each month, which enabled the old lady, when she filled out forms, to describe herself as "Emilie Manu, property owner."

Had not Emile's mother put up a brass plate by the front door on which, beneath her name, were the words Piano Teacher, when in reality she had no formal training whatsoever and knew only just enough to teach beginners or to give a smattering of musical culture to young ladies who had nothing better to do?

And those steaks that were always too small and too thin, but that were always put on his plate with the ritual phrase, "You need building up . . ."

How could you expect an examining magistrate to understand things like that? Or anyone else in the court, for that matter?

Yet Loursat understood, and a smile flitted across his face.

"The inquiry has established that up to last autumn the accused had only one friend, a certain Justin Luska, whom he had been to school with and who worked for Prisunic, situated on the opposite side of the street to the Librairie Georges. Formerly the two boys had been in the same class of the public school. It is worth noting that Manu, the good student, the fast learner, was highly thought of . . . Luska, on the other hand, because of his red hair, his name—his real first name was Ephraïm—his father's Eastern origin, was an object of ridicule.

"Two children, two temperaments that had already formed,

Luska, gentle, patient, submitting without a word to the gross and often brutal jokes."

Yes, this was all factually correct. Except that Ducup, of course, didn't really understand any of it. It was true that Luska, to learn his trade, hadn't been ashamed to wait on customers at a stall on the sidewalk, to be a hawker, as they say.

He was always badly dressed but didn't seem to care. People said that he smelled of his father's shop, but he didn't take offense when people made fun of him. The owners of the Prisunic didn't allow their outdoor salesmen to wear overcoats or gloves, as that might have aroused the pity of the customers. So all through the winter he had to wear two sweaters underneath his jacket.

"The evidence will show that the accused repeatedly begged Luska to introduce him to a group of young people who, to use a somewhat hackneyed phrase, might be described as the gilded youth of this town.

"It rained on the night that the introduction was to take place. Manu had planned to meet his friend at eight o'clock outside Tellier's, the watchmaker's on the rue d'Allier. He had to wait a considerable time as Luska's mother was having heart trouble that evening and her son was sent to fetch a doctor.

"The two young men went to the Boxing Bar, which was the regular meeting place of the group I have mentioned..."

Loursat, who had seemed to be dozing, slowly looked up. He knew that Ducup was getting onto very thin ice, and he listened with interest.

"No complaints had been registered, the police did not call to account certain acts and pranks of the members of the group. Suffice it to say that these young people have allowed themselves to be influenced by certain books and films, against which they lacked the moral strength to resist."

And Ducup, pleased with his finesse, continued, "Young people in every age have engaged in hero-worship. The oldest among us will recall the appeal of the dashing cavalry officer! And now that we live, as it were, in the age of the gangster, it is hardly surprising that . . ."

Loursat muttered into his beard, "Idiot!"

There was some truth in this depiction, but it was far too pat! He, the obese Loursat, was the only one among these marionettes who really understood what had gone on.

Loursat had had nothing to drink that morning. He was longing for the lunchtime adjournment, when he would be able to have his two or three glasses of red wine. Now and then he felt a reawakening of contempt and irritation, the kind that left a bad taste in his mouth every morning.

When he had been a boy himself, he'd hardly been conscious of the existence of people like this Emile Manu, poor, eager for life, yet frustrated at every turn.

Had he noticed anything of the life that went on around him? He had lived like a character in a tragedy, surrounded by high-minded sentiments. When he had loved he had done so without reservation, without doubt, without bending to the demands of reality.

It was extraordinary to think of it there in that courtroom, which had existed in those days and in which just the same human dramas had been enacted.

Yet he had noticed nothing. The town must have been what it was now, and there must have been Rogissarts and Ducups, people like his sister Marthe and Dossin, setting the social tone. There must have been poor people and bars like Joe's and women prowling the sidewalks.

He had lived in an ideal world, blending study and love. Never mind, he *had* loved! His love had been buried deeply inside him, but it was no less real. What was the point of acting a part, of indulging in demonstrations of affection that were always more or less grotesque?

He had kissed his wife and then returned to his books,

meeting her again at the next meal. When she was pregnant, he was happy. Once the baby was born he had looked into the nursery three or four times a day.

To put it into language Ducup could understand, it was a traditional time, a period when everything seemed to be in its proper place: the Palais de Justice, the Prefecture, the Town Hall, the church! The magistrates too, the lawyers, the *haute bourgeoisie*, and beneath them the people one didn't know, the *petite bourgeoisie*, the people who streamed from their homes in the mornings to go to work in the shops and offices.

That period had ended abruptly the day Geneviève had gone off with Bernard!

As for him, instead of whining or fulminating, he had at a stroke obliterated everything, wiped the slate clean.

Imbeciles! A whole town of fools, of wretched human beings who didn't know why they were alive, who were moved along like cattle, complete with yoke and bell!

The town itself was no more than a barren landscape which stretched out on all sides of the dark little burrow, warmed with a little stove, furnished with books and bottles of burgundy, in which henceforward Hector Loursat was to live aloof in haughty isolation.

What were the magistrates? . . . Idiots!

The lawyers? Ditto. And what's more, many of them were shysters!

All of them idiots!

The Dossins, whose one thought was to have a smarter house than anyone else in the town and who, to make sure of it, had revived the custom, long disused, of being waited on by a butler in white gloves!

Rogissart, who went on his pilgrimages in the hope of persuading Providence to give him a son as tall and rangy as himself!

Ducup, who would "get somewhere," because he had taken the necessary steps!

And on the other hand, a purring stove, dark red wine, and all the books you could wish. He had read everything, he knew everything, and he could afford to sit in his own corner and sneer, "The fools!"

And he was often inclined to add, "Pestilent fools!"

Then—crack! A pistol shot on the floor above. A gang of young people were discovered, and within twenty-four hours he had left his lair to go scurrying in their wake.

To discover a new world, new people, new sounds and smells, new thoughts, new feelings, a swarming, writhing world, which had no relation to the epics and tragedies of literature, one that was full of all those mysterious and generally trivial details you don't find in books—the breath of cold air in a dirty back alley, the loiterer on a street corner, a shop remaining open long after all others had closed, an impatient, highly strung boy waiting all keyed up outside a watchmaker's for the friend who was going to lead him into a new and unknown future.

From time to time he shifted his position with so audible a grunt that everyone turned to look at him, including Ducup, who was afraid of losing the thread of his discourse, even though he knew it practically by heart.

No one could understand why he, Loursat, was there at all. He could easily have taken a trip or to his bed, at least that's what Marthe had suggested. Hadn't she herself been sick? And hadn't her son needed to convalesce in the mountains of Switzerland?

Dossin had pleaded with him too, and Rogissart, after months of frigid silence, had been to see him too, appealing to him both as a cousin and as a magistrate.

But there he was, on the bench for the defense. And many eyes were turned on him more accusingly than on the accused. Anxiously too, wondering what he would find to say when Nicole's name was brought in, as it was bound to be.

Ducup led up to the subject cautiously. "What's convinced

me that these young people were more imprudent than blame-worthy is the fact that, after Emile Manu's accident, they did not consider for a moment leaving the injured man on the road, in spite of their having been placed in a dangerous situation ...Unfortunately I am unable to associate the accused with that attitude since he admits that he was at that moment vomiting by the side of the road, and hardly knew what was going on.

"Mademoiselle Nicole Loursat showed kindness and presence of mind. She suggested that he should be taken to her home."

Loursat was tempted to chime in with a rude word, to repeat like some sort of madman, "Not true!"

But he contented himself with a scornful look. It wasn't true. Nicole, he well knew, had not been motivated by kindness at all but by a practical common sense that did not leave her even when she was inwardly most perplexed.

The truth was that every one of them had been tight that night. He had questioned them all, and there wasn't one who could give a really coherent account of what had happened. The drenching rain had added to the general confusion. Emile, who had a horror of blood, had thrown up under a tree.

A car had passed in the opposite direction, and the driver had poured out a stream of abuse at them for leaving their vehicle in the middle of the road.

Before they reached him, Big Louie had moved. They didn't know who he was. In the glow of the red taillight they could see a figure struggling to get to his feet, his face bloodied, his eyes haggard, his leg twisted at a strange angle. He began shouting at them, "Don't go! ... Don't go! ... I need help!"

And it was partly to keep him quiet that they ran over to him.

"You sure got me, you bastards!" he said to them. "Take me someplace, but not to a hospital ... no cops ... hear me? Who are you? Shit ... you're just kids!"

In fact it was he who had given the orders! That was as near as possible the true story of what had happened. At least it was the most plausible version of it that Loursat had been able to piece together from conflicting accounts.

Daillat had lifted the man's shoulders and Destrivaux his feet, and before they reached the car the latter had lost his glasses. They had forgotten all about Emile and almost driven off without him. Luckily someone remembered him in time. He had been found prostrate at the foot of a tree, and he too had had to be carried to the car.

Most of this would come out when Nicole went into the witness-box. Only, of course, there'd be no talk about the kindness of her heart! She would answer questions simply just as she had done before the examining magistrate.

"It was his idea. He didn't want to be taken to the hospital and he told us to say nothing about it to the police. Edmond noticed he was tattooed."

"Who brought the doctor?"

"Edmond. We thought he should be the one to go since he knew the doctor best."

What Dr. Matray would say could also be predicted, since it was all down in folder no. 17.

"I first of all thought that the injured man was alone with Mademoiselle Loursat and Edmond Dossin. Then I saw the door of the next room open slightly. I gradually discovered that there was a whole group of young people there. They were scared and highly excited. One of them was lying on the floor, and I advised them to let him sleep, because he was obviously drunk."

Poor Dr. Matray, who attended all the best families in Moulins, and who looked for all the world like the hero in a Jules Verne novel!

"I tried to establish the attitude of all of those present that night," Ducup continued, occasionally cracking his fingers to relieve the numbness.

Not true! It was Loursat who had done that!

"Mademoiselle Loursat displayed great strength of character, and, on the instructions of Dr. Matray, acted the perfect nurse."

My God! Nicole had only behaved mechanically, and that's what made her seem so composed.

"Monsieur Edmond Dossin, worried, asked the doctor for advice...As he will testify later..."

Testify what? That it wasn't his fault! That he was prepared to pay for the wounded man to go to a clinic! That he had offered to get a friend of his father, who was in the government, to take action on behalf of Big Louie?

Finally Destrivaux, who had lost his glasses, and could only squint at all these events with his shortsighted gaze.

Imagine if Loursat had been put in the witness-box! When asked whether he hadn't heard them carry Big Louie upstairs he wouldn't have bothered talking about the long corridors, the staircases, the two wings of his house, but would have answered bluntly, "No, Gentlemen of the Jury. I was drunk!"

Not that it was true. He had been, as on other evenings, comfortable, warm, drowsy, and protected in his solitude.

The members of the jury did their best to look serious and detached under public scrutiny, for half the people in court knew who they were. The crowd was getting restless. They'd had enough of Ducup and were eager to come to the real business. Someone went up and whispered to Rogissart, who sat with a box of peppermints in front of him. It wasn't hard to guess what was said:

"She hasn't been found yet."

The Pigasse woman! For that was how Adèle would be referred to in the court.

Rogissart looked at his cousin and shook his head as if to say, "No. No sign of her yet—though we're doing all we can."

Ducup's mouth was getting dry, his delivery less glib. He

tried not to see Loursat, who sat huddled up, compact, Mephistophelian.

"It seems to have been in the course of that night, at approximately four A.M., that an attachment was formed between the accused and Mademoiselle Nicole Loursat."

The very subject they were all trying to avoid! Not just for Loursat's sake, but for the sake of his family, his colleagues, the whole of Moulins society!

He, however, wanted it all out on display! If only they knew what was making him smile at that precise moment. That morning, before setting off for court, he had almost shaved off his beard! That would have shocked them. He would have turned up clean-shaven, with his hair combed and a spotless collar!

"In the course of his third interrogation, which took place on October eighteenth, the accused informed me that, if he had begged his friend Luska to introduce him to the group, it was because he had already fallen in love with Mademoiselle Loursat . . . In this way, he seeks to explain the fact that, on awakening, still in a drunken stupor, he burst out passionately . . .

"Mlle Loursat states for her part that he was bitterly ashamed of what had happened and of the filthy mess he was in. He begged her forgiveness and then proceeded to pour out his feelings, telling her it was for her that he had joined them in the Boxing Bar that night."

As a witness, Ducup was not entitled to make use of notes. His memory was astonishing, though the effort was visible at times, when he would pause and shut his eyes, trying to recall the exact words that had been recorded.

"From that day onward, Manu came to the house as often as circumstances would permit. I won't say that he profited by the accident, but it certainly provided good cover. Meanwhile . . ."

Ducup was far off the mark. He'd never been eighteen, never been in love, or ambitious. The same could be said of Loursat.

But at least he could sense what eighteen was like for others!

"He came by every evening, I might say every night, since he often got back to his mother's house at three in the morning. He used to sneak in like a thief through the back door which opens onto l'impasse des Tanneurs..."

No. Not like a thief! At the moment, however, Loursat's thoughts were far away, so distant that he almost took out a cigarette and lit it.

"To all my questions on his relations with Mademoiselle Loursat, the accused replied cynically: 'I refuse to go into the details of my private life.'

"But he didn't deny that he took advantage of the intimacy created by the accident to visit the young lady's room frequently—"

They had heard Loursat. "You will make the stain of punishment worse than it is...you are sure to cause a scandal..."

They were all looking at Loursat, who turned his large eyes back at them, smiling complacently beneath his moustache.

"If there's the least disturbance, I'll clear the court," the president shouted as a murmur of curiosity and excitement rose in the courtroom.

Ducup began again. His head was hot and his hands cold, and he would be as glad as anyone when his evidence was finished. "Twelve days later, the crime was committed. It is to establish what was done, during that period, by the usual inhabitants of the house, that this court..."

In Loursat's case there wasn't much to tell. He had his stove, his burgundy, the old books he chose at random from the shelves, reading three or fifty pages, refilling his glass, enveloped in the warm atmosphere until he turned in at night.

"On the relations of the accused with Mademoiselle Loursat it is unnecessary to..."

But why was it unnecessary? Nicole and Emile were lovers. On the third night, to be exact, and every night thereafter! The boy proud and feverishly happy, though gnawed at by terrible misgivings, the girl swept off her feet by his ardor.

They loved each other, and, as far as they were concerned, the whole town could go to blazes provided they could be together...

And the other young people, who had unknowingly brought the pair together—Edmond, Daillat, Destrivaux, Luska, the lawyer Grouin's boy—they were mere props, vague figures that stood in the lovers' way. Even Big Louie, who had the least chance to find an alibi, an excuse, a reason for being there.

It was because it had all begun with such violence—in mud, blood, and vomit—that everything had rushed to a climax. And here was the pallid Ducup cutting it all up into thin slices for the court.

Loursat's thirst was becoming unbearable. Ducup had hardly come to the end of his final sentence before the lawyer rose from his seat, like a schoolboy who wants permission to leave a classroom, to say, "Might I suggest, Monsieur le Président, that an adjournment at this stage..."

And the sitting ended in the scrape of chairs and shuffle of feet.

10

THAT afternoon everyone settled in his place with satisfaction. People looked around, nudged their neighbors, and smirked. The president, M. Niquet, glanced proudly at the stove he had had installed in record time, a monumental affair with fifteen feet of piping, ending in an elbow that disappeared out one of the windows. It smoked a bit, but no one worried; the fire had, after all, only just been lit.

In fact everybody was comfortably installed and only waiting for the fun to start.

"If the defense has no objection, we'll take Destrivaux's evidence first. He has been given special leave, with instructions to return to his unit as soon as possible."

The young man pushed his way through the crowd, apologizing right and left. The court was packed; even the lawyers were squeezed in remote corners of the room.

The president was really pleased with himself. His absurd grin became more monstrous than ever as he beamed at the jury, then at his two assessors, one on either hand, then at the prosecutor. "We're all friends here, aren't we?" he seemed to be saying. "And now that we've got that stove . . ."

Out loud and in a paternal voice he said to Destrivaux, "Now turn toward the jury, please. Don't be afraid."

The former bank clerk looked an absolute scarecrow in the voluminous folds of his ill-fitting uniform, gathered in at the waist by a leather belt.

"You are not related to, or in the employ of, the defendant in any way? Repeat after me: 'I swear to tell the truth, the whole truth...'"

Loursat couldn't help smiling at Emile Manu as the boy gazed at his former comrade, amazed at his transformation. Just then, there was a disturbance at the back of the court. It was Destrivaux's father, who put his hand to his face to stifle a sob, then rose dramatically to head for the exit, unable to bear the proceedings any longer.

The crowd settled down. The president examined his documents. "You were one of Emile Manu's comrades in a group of young people who used to meet in the Boxing Bar?"

"I was."

"Were you there on the evening of September twenty-third?"

"Yes, Your Honor."

He spoke quietly and with becoming reverence, as to his officers.

"Did you know the accused previously?"

"Only by sight, Your Honor."

"Ah, by sight. Isn't true that you lived on the same street? And you weren't pals—not friends at all?"

One would have thought the president had made some major discovery, such was the relish with which he continued his line of questioning. "And didn't you both work in town? Wouldn't you have often left home at about the same hour?"

"I always went to work on my bicycle, Your Honor."

"I see! You have a bicycle! Was there any particular reason you might have wished not to know him?"

"No...I can't think of any."

"What impression did the accused make on you when he joined your group?"

"No impression either way, Your Honor."

"Did he appear to be shy?"

"No, Your Honor."

"Didn't you notice anything about him at all?"

"He didn't know how to play cards."

"Did you teach him? What game did you play?"

"Ecarté . . . It was Edmond who taught him to play and won fifty francs from him."

"Was your friend Edmond Dossin generally lucky at cards?"

The answer came quite candidly, "No. It wasn't luck. He cheated."

He was disconcerted for a moment by the roar of laughter that burst out. As for the crowd, they were really beginning to enjoy themselves.

"Ah! He cheated, you say! Did he often cheat?"

"Always. He was quite frank about it."

"Then why did people play with him?"

"To find out how he did it."

Rogissart exchanged glances with one of the assistants, who was known all over Moulins as a first-rate amateur conjurer. The president looked at them, puzzled, wondering what they were silently conversing about.

"Did you have much to drink that evening?"

"The same as usual."

"How much would that be?"

"Five or six glasses."

"What of?"

"Cognac mixed with Pernod."

Another laugh, starting at the front row and spreading to the back. Only Emile remained deadly serious, listening with his chin resting on his hand, staring hard at the witness so as not to miss a word.

"Who proposed the trip to the Auberge aux Noyés?"

"I don't remember."

An impatient gesture from Emile, which clearly meant "Liar!"

"Had you been there before?"

"Several times."

"And on other occasions how did you get there?"

"In Daillat's truck... Or rather, his father's. But that night it had been taken to Nevers to pick up some pigs."

"Was it Manu's idea to grab the first car you found?"

"We may have encouraged him a bit."

"Who do you mean by 'we'?"

"All of us, I guess."

He had meant to be absolutely honest, and he was making an effort. He knew he had slipped, though. If he had been telling the truth, he would have answered: "We filled him up with liquor and then dared him to pinch a car." But those words just wouldn't come out.

"So the accused drove you all to the Auberge aux Noyés. What happened then?"

"We had some drinks. Mostly white wine. They only had that and beer... We danced."

"Did Manu dance?"

"Yes. With Nicole."

"If I'm not mistaken, there were two young ladies at the inn: Eva and Clara. What did you do with them?"

M. Niquet was rather scared of the answer he might receive; at the same time he was proud of himself for asking so daring a question.

"We pawed them a bit."

"Nothing more?"

"Not as far as I was concerned."

"And the others?"

"I don't know... I didn't see anyone go upstairs."

Smiles this time and a faint titter. For Emile Manu and Destrivaux, though, these things were too simple and familiar to seem amusing.

"I am not going to ask you to describe the accident. We have ample evidence to establish the facts, which are in any case not disputed...Now tell me, did you often go to Mademoiselle Loursat's house?"

"Yes...Often."

"To drink and dance? Weren't you ever afraid the young girl's father might appear?"

What was so strange was the way Destrivaux looked questioningly at Emile, as much as to say, "What should I answer?"

"We'll let that pass," said the president. "To come now to this Louis Gagalin, better known as Big Louie—did his presence make any change in your habits?"

"We were afraid."

"Ah! Afraid he might involve you in a scandal?"

"Not exactly...We were afraid of him."

Loursat heaved a sigh. How dense this old Niquet was! Had he forgotten all about childhood and its fears? Of course they were afraid. They had been playing cops and robbers and suddenly they found the real thing in their midst! A great tattooed brute who had committed real crimes and been in prison.

Big Louie wouldn't have been slow to see it either. What children he must have thought them, with their silly little thefts of coffeepots and pumpkins.

"I want you to think carefully before answering this...Was there ever any question among you, any talk, either at the house or at the Boxing Bar or elsewhere, of your getting rid of Big Louie by one means or another?"

"Yes, Your Honor."

"Who spoke of getting rid of him?"

"I can't remember...We just thought that, now that he'd found his meal ticket, he could go on blackmailing us forever."

"And there was talk of killing him?"

"Yes."

"Was the subject discussed seriously?"

Of course not seriously! Loursat fidgeted on his bench. This whole line of questioning was pointless. They didn't understand that young people could discuss a crime down to the smallest detail just for the fun of it, without the slightest intention of following through on it.

"Maître Loursat . . . Have you any questions which you wish to put to the witness?"

"Yes, Monsieur le Président . . . I would like you to ask him who besides Emile Manu was in love with Nicole."

"You heard the question, Destrivaux . . . I know the situation is rather peculiar, but you must recognize that the query comes from the counsel for the defense . . . Answer."

"I don't know."

"Allow me, Monsieur le Président . . . Before the arrival of Manu, did Nicole pair off with anybody?"

"With Edmond Dossin."

"They pretended to be sweethearts, but it was really a game, wasn't it? Did you ever get the impression that anyone else in the gang really cared for her?"

"I thought Luska might."

"Did he tell you so himself?"

"No. He was never very communicative."

"Was it as a result of the accident and the fact that there was an injured man in the house that the group appeared to be breaking up?"

No answer from Destrivaux, and Loursat went on:

"Or was it rather that Nicole had now a real lover?"

People craned their necks to look at Destrivaux, who looked down awkwardly, not knowing what to say.

"That's all, Your Honor."

"Any further questions from the prosecution?"

"No further questions."

"I assume neither side is likely to wish to recall the witness? . . . In that case, he may rejoin his regiment . . . Thank you, young man."

He would have liked to keep the witness in the box longer. He knew what was coming, and though he had prepared himself for it, he nonetheless dreaded it.

"Call in Mademoiselle Nicole Loursat."

He glanced apologetically at Loursat, who, however, was in need of no sympathy. As he watched her make her way to the witness-box he looked more like a proud father than anything else:

"...the truth, the whole truth..."

She was duly sworn in.

"You stated to the examining magistrate that on the night of the eighth of October the accused was in your room."

"Yes, Your Honor."

She had smiled at Emile, simply and with perfect self-possession.

"Did you both go up to see the injured man?"

"No, Your Honor. I went there at about nine o'clock—to take up Big Louie's dinner."

"So it wasn't to help you look after Big Louie that he came to the house."

"No, Your Honor."

"Then I hardly need to dwell on his reasons for being there ...Did you expect any of the others that evening?"

"No. Their visits had become rarer and rarer. I hadn't seen any of them for some days."

"Do you know why?"

"I think they realized we preferred to be alone."

The crowd looked at Loursat even more than at her. He would have liked to smile at them.

"When did the accused leave?"

"At twenty to twelve. I wanted him to get to bed early as he was looking rather exhausted."

"You call that early?"

"It was generally after two when he left."

Rogissart was fiddling with his propeller pencil, gazing at it intently.

"Did you talk about Big Louie that evening?"

"We might have, but I don't remember it."

"When Manu left your room, it was ostensibly to go home. Yet a few minutes later your father saw him coming downstairs from the second floor. Is that correct?"

"Yes."

"How do you explain that?"

"He has told you. He heard a noise and went up."

The president had a whispered conversation with his two assistants. All three shrugged their shoulders. A glance at Rogissart, who shook his head, then at Loursat.

"Thank you. You may step down."

With a little bow to the judges, she left the witness-box. Having given her evidence, she was allowed to sit just behind her father, so that she could help him with his manila folders. The president coughed; Rogissart nearly broke the lead in his pencil. The crowd stirred expectantly, sensing their discomfort but unable to guess its cause.

"Bring in the next witness—Edmond Dossin."

He came armed with a medical certificate saying that he was in a very delicate state of health and requesting the court not to submit him to a more prolonged examination than was absolutely necessary.

He was pale and looked more effeminate than ever. That didn't seem to bother him, however, and he glanced disdainfully at the prisoner in the dock.

"Tell the jury what you know of the incidents . . . Speak up, please!"

"We were supposed to return the objects, like at Aix."

"You mean to say that at Aix-les-Bains, where you played the same game, you returned the stolen objects to their owners?"

"Every morning, we left them outside the place we took

them from, and the police found them . . . At Moulins we decided to collect a hoard—mainly because we had a whole attic at our disposal."

"In your uncle's house. In your opinion, what was the attitude of the accused to all this?"

"He took everything seriously. Right from the start I told the others he'd be trouble."

Loursat didn't seem to be listening. He sat in a heap with his arms folded and his head sunk on his chest, and anybody might have thought he was asleep. Indeed one of the assistants nudged the president.

"Did the accused appear to you to be scared by the turn of events?"

"Scared stiff. Particularly by Big Louie's demands for money."

"Do you know where the accused got the money?"

No response. Nicole had been checking through the folders, and handed her father a sheet of paper.

"Would you kindly ask the witness, Your Honor, if he had had relations with the Pigasse woman?"

"Did you hear the question? . . . You may answer."

"Yes. That is to say . . ."

"How many times?"

"Once."

The stove was still smoking. The hands of the clock on the wall behind the tribunal marched slowly onward. And like a low hum the same legal formulas seemed to have lost all meaning and become a background sound. "Please address the jury . . . Any more questions, Maître?"

Loursat had a start, for he was thinking about something else. At that precise moment he was thinking that his nephew Edmond would not live to be old, that he had at best another two or three years. Why? Just an impression. Now he stared at him with his large, soft eyes, the look he had when he was getting to the heart of the matter.

Any questions? No. What was the use? He had a manila folder full of questions—and answers—on everything, including Edmond's movements on the night of October 7th.

Not that it was all necessarily true.

Edmond had been in the Boxing Bar till nearly half past eleven, and then Destrivaux had walked him to his door.

Supposing Edmond had killed Big Louie? It was conceivable, but the same could be said of Destrivaux or any of the others. Of Emile too!

After all, it was only a question of carrying their game to its logical conclusion.

How was it then that Loursat had from the start been convinced of Emile's innocence? He had observed him when Edmond had been in the witness-box. The boy's eyes, fixed on the witness, had been full of hatred.

He must have hated him from the start. For being rich and well dressed, for being the leader of the gang, for taking Nicole under his wing, for belonging to one of the best families in the town.

And his hatred must have been returned, though Edmond's reasons would be just the opposite.

It was not, however, by the monotonous sequence of question and answer that you can make things of that sort understandable to a pack of stolid jurymen.

"When you heard of the murder of Big Louie, did you think first of all of Emile Manu?"

"I don't know."

"Did you think of anyone else in your group?"

"I don't know...No...I don't think so."

After all the young people had been cross-examined, things would begin to move more quickly. But the president insisted on carrying out his duties to the letter.

"Just now, your friend Destrivaux expressed his regret and

remorse at having allowed himself to be dragged into such dangerous ways. For your part, do you..."

And Edmond complied:

"I'm sorry."

But not like Destrivaux, who had prepared his speech in advance and recited it to the letter: "I regret everything I have done and am sorry for the shame I have brought on my family, which has only ever provided a good example to me. I ask pardon for the harm I have done and..."

Another whole hour of evidence by the light of the big yellow globes that threw a harsh light on the faces of the principal figures but left the further parts of the courtroom in shadow, as in the remoter corners of a church.

In the witnesses' room Angèle told lurid stories of what went on at night in the Loursats' house, undismayed by the presence of Phine, who sat with pursed lips, looking the other way, pretending not to hear.

Hour after hour the unreality of a court of law had gradually taken hold of the listeners, so that, on leaving the Palais de Justice, it was the real world outside, the street lamps, the frosty pavements, the passing cars and pedestrians that now seemed unfamiliar, unreal.

Joe fell into step by Loursat's side. "I wonder where she's gone," he said. "I've been all round the place, looking high and low, without finding a trace of her... How do you think it's going?... The trial, I mean... Strikes me we're not doing too badly, though of course I wouldn't know."

On the way home, Phine bought some provisions for a cold supper. The house seemed more than normally empty and cheerless.

They hardly knew what to do with themselves. They seemed to have one foot in ordinary life, the other still in court.

Nicole ate nevertheless with apparent appetite. Several times

Loursat caught her eye and each time looked away quickly. If he knew what she was thinking, he preferred that she not speak about it.

It was some time now since she had started looking at him like that. It was a look of curiosity, mixed perhaps with admiration and certainly with other elements—a shy gratitude and a still shyer affection which did not yet dare to assert itself.

In a voice that was intended to be casual, she asked, as they got up from the table, "What are you doing this evening?"

"Nothing...I think I'll get to bed early."

It wasn't true...He knew perfectly well she was worried, and why, but he couldn't very well promise her he wouldn't drink.

Besides, he needed to drink, to drink all alone behind his padded door, to smoke one cigarette after another, to poke the fire in the little stove, to sit down, to get up and wander about, to grunt and mutter to himself, and to run his fingers through his hair.

Three times she came and listened anxiously at his door. He was quite aware of her presence, yet he didn't open it.

Round and round his room he plodded, and his thoughts, plodding too, went round and round in circles, always coming back to the same point.

One of the gang had shot Big Louie. Whoever it was knew that he was a murderer and that Emile was innocent. He had known it all along. Yet he had faced the examining magistrate squarely, producing a convincing alibi, be it his bed or elsewhere.

He had faced Ducup, he had faced Loursat, but that had only left him face to face with himself. That was the worst of all.

It was to escape that unbearable solitude that he had wandered about the streets at night and had sought consolation with Adèle Pigasse.

Each time in the relief of that factitious intimacy he had almost broken down. He had wanted to tell her.

He had resisted. He had returned. He had resisted again... Finally he had succumbed. He had got the evil load off his chest.

How had he done it? Boastfully? Sneeringly? Or owning up to his panic?

And Loursat had looked him in the eye! He had talked to all of them. He had seen nothing. Destrivaux, who tried so hard to please everybody, and Dossin, so happy to escape his responsibilities because he was ill. He seemed to be saying:

"You can see that I'm weak, and that I don't have long to live. I was just having fun, none of it really mattered."

The following morning they'd have Daillat in the witness box, then Luska, whose father had wilted visibly during the last three months.

Some church bells were ringing. Adèle and Gène were tucked away somewhere. Surely they must know they were wanted.

Ten times the lawyer went to his cupboard and poured out some rum. At first it was only a few drops; after that, each time a little more. He went to bed glowing, feeling that just a little more effort was required. Yet would that effort be forthcoming—at just the right moment, of course? It might all turn on a single word.

The Rogissarts were happy. The trial had gone well. They'd managed to gloss over certain things. Indeed, the Bear hadn't behaved too badly, all things considered, and Nicole, if she had appeared completely unrepentant, had at any rate been fairly discreet. Naturally there was plenty of telephoning. Dossin, for instance, rang up to know whether Edmond was out of the woods or whether any of the witnesses were likely to refer to him. The boy himself had been put to bed with a temperature, and his mother—on her feet for once—was fussing around him. As for Luska, he had locked himself up in his room, which wasn't a real room at all, but a sort of shed in the backyard.

In the rue Ernest-Voivenon, Mme Manu prayed, then wept, then prayed again. At ten o'clock she went to see that the front door was properly bolted, for she was nervous at night, and after that she wept again as she undressed and went to bed.

Next morning, soon after eight o'clock, the streets were once again full of people converging on the Palais de Justice. In the courtroom, people were already on nodding terms with their neighbors, though they hadn't yet got so far as shaking hands with them.

Emile had on the same suit and the same tie. He hadn't slept much, and the effect of fatigue was to make him look less candid than on the previous day.

Loursat was surprised not to see Joe. He was scheduled to give testimony that morning.

"Gentlemen, the Court!"

Daillat was called to the witness-box and sworn in. He wore a brown suit. His florid face was covered with freckles and his hair was cropped short like a soldier's. He at any rate was not impressed by the solemnity of the occasion. He studied the people on the public benches and, when he caught sight of a friend, he winked.

"You are a butcher in the employ of your father, and at the deposition you declared that you took several hams from the stock."

He responded glibly, "If I hadn't told you myself, you'd never have figured it out."

"You also took money from the cashbox. Do you mean you stole from your father?"

"Of course I did. It's a family business. If the rest of them help themselves, why shouldn't I?"

"It seems to me that your father—"

"The books never add up, and every night my mother yells. Well, what's a bit more?"

"You met up with the accused at the Boxing Bar the night of the accident and..."

Loursat was aware of something behind him. Turning around, he saw someone signaling to him from the third row, unable to get any closer because of the bank of lawyers. Loursat didn't recognize him, but he was doubtless connected with Joe.

Loursat rose and moved toward him. "It's urgent," the other whispered, passing him a crumpled envelope.

The president's questions went on while Loursat tore open the grubby letter. He was aware of Rogissart's eyes, turned on him a little anxiously.

I've found them. It would be a dirty trick to drag them into court now. There are some things I didn't know about Gène and he's got to lay low. I promised you'd leave them in peace if Adèle said who did it and she said it was Luska. Now you know, you'll be able to get it out of him somehow or other. You don't need her. I know you'll do your best.—Joe.

The president was leaning forward.

"I asked you, Maître Loursat."

"I beg your pardon, Monsieur le Président... No. No questions."

Daillat was dismissed. Emile, looking absolutely washed out, sat limply in his seat.

"The next witness... Justin Luska."

The stove still smoked a bit. One of the jurymen was getting the fumes right in the face. He held his head back with a disgusted look, and used his handkerchief as a fan.

Loursat, leaning on his elbows, with his eyes shut, waited patiently.

II

WEDGED up against the wall near a bunch of lawyers stood a man who was quite unlike any of his neighbors. A different breed altogether, a man belonging to that race of humans that you find sleeping in the corridors of night trains, sitting patiently in police stations, waiting anxiously for their papers to be examined, or trying desperately to explain themselves in a mixture of languages, the sort that travel with indescribable baggage tied up with cord, that are dragged protesting out of trains at border crossings, and who are always bullied by officials.

Perhaps it is for just that reason that they have those big, piteous, pleading eyes, like those of a deer.

If he smelled a bit, it was probably only his corduroy jacket, but nobody would think of that. In any case he was quite oblivious of it himself, so it didn't really matter. Pushed this way and that he stood on tiptoe gazing straight in front of him, stupidly, or it may have been fanatically, at all events without the slightest sign of being aware of his surroundings. His face was adorned with a heavy drooping moustache, like a typical Bulgarian's, and it would have been easy to imagine him in national costume, or at any rate with metal buttons on his vest, strange boots and earrings, holding a whip in his hand.

It is true that President Niquet, with his head split in half by his mouth, looked like a cynical, scolding ventriloquist's dummy. But what was he saying? Loursat was listening. Certain phrases registered without his being conscious of them.

"...born at Batum on the..."

It was all in the dossier. This must be Luska's father. He'd been born in Batum, that far-away city at the foot of the Caucasus, in which twenty-eight different nationalities jostle each other. Had his grandfather worn silk clothes, a turban, or a fez? However that may be, the family had one day started to wander, as it had no doubt done many times before, seeking greener pastures. At the age of ten he had been living in Constantinople, two years later in the rue Saint-Paul in Paris.

He was dark and oily, while his son, who now stood in the witness-box, had a tinge of red in his frizzy hair, which rose in a series of levels from his forehead.

"I got to know Edmond Dossin one evening when I was playing billiards in the Brasserie de la République."

The president too must have wondered how this humble sidewalk vendor could have hooked himself onto the smart set of the town. But Ducup had explained it plausibly enough. Even the *grands seigneurs* need their courtiers, and this Luska could be relied on to laugh when he ought to laugh, to applaud, to flatter, and to fall in with the whims of his betters.

"How long ago was that?"

"I don't know exactly...Sometime last winter."

"Speak up, will you?...The jury wants to hear you."

"Sometime last winter."

Loursat frowned. He had caught sight of the boy's father and for the last five minutes he had been staring at him, as though by doing so he would be able to understand all the...

Suddenly he seemed to wake up with a start. He turned to Nicole and said something in a low voice. While she rummaged in the folders, he turned to look at the witness, trying, like a latecomer at Mass, to guess just where they'd got to.

"Yes," said Nicole, "he's down to give evidence. You put him down yourself."

He got to his feet regardless of the fact that he was interrupting a question.

"Excuse me, Monsieur le Président!...It has just come to my notice that a witness who has still to give evidence is present in the court."

Everyone looked around the courtroom, trying to guess who it was. And strangely, Luska's father himself looked around puzzled, as if preferring not to realize it was him that Loursat was referring to.

"To whom do you refer, Maître Loursat?"

"To Ephraïm Luska, the father of the present witness. He is standing over there behind a group of my colleagues."

Meanwhile the offender's son stood awkwardly in the witness-box not knowing what to do with his hands.

"Ephraïm Luska!...Why aren't you in the witnesses' room? How did you get here?"

The man stood rigid, holding his breath, hoping against hope that he had heard wrong and that it wasn't to him that the words were being addressed. The man with the big pathetic eyes pointed vaguely toward a door that he had certainly not come through. He didn't understand why he was there, or how, and he threaded his way past the rows, murmuring words to himself as he headed to the room he ought to have been in.

"Let's get back to our flock."

M. Niquet said that without thinking of the witness's woolly hair and for a moment he couldn't understand what the laughter was about. When he did, he flushed.

"Any questions, Monsieur l'Advocat Général?"

The Advocat Général was the prosecutor, Rogissart.

"I would like you to ask the witness, who had known the accused ever since they were at school together, whether he would describe him as of a frank and good-natured disposition or on the other hand reserved and quick to take offense?"

At first Emile Manu had been too self-conscious under the

eyes of the public to behave naturally, but by this time he had almost forgotten their existence. As the question was asked, he thrust out his chin and looked threateningly at his former friend.

Luska, for his part, had instinctively turned toward the dock, and he looked still more darkly at Emile.

"He's always been easily offended."

He certainly was this time! His features were twisted into an angry sneer and he glanced at the jury as though calling upon them to witness the enormity of the suggestion. For a moment it looked as though he would spring to his feet.

"When you were at school together, you knew what sort of a home he came from?"

"Yes."

"Now I want you to think carefully before answering this... Do you consider him to have been envious of those who were better off than himself? Manu lived in modest circumstances, as did you. At school, students formed cliques... jealousies grew, became hatreds."

Emile shouted, "What are you—?"

"Silence!... Don't interrupt the witness."

It was the first time Emile had lost control of himself. He didn't calm down for a moment and went on muttering till the president turned on him again.

"Silence!... Allow the witness to speak."

"Yes, Monsieur le Président."

"You mean you consider he was envious?"

"Yes."

"You said just now that it was you who introduced Manu to the group in the Boxing Bar... Now what was his attitude to Edmond Dossin, Destrivaux, and Daillat?"

"I could see he didn't take to them."

"Right. He didn't take to them... Did he say or do anything to show his dislike?"

"He accused Edmond of cheating."

Emile was so wound up it looked as if he might leap over the rail at any point.

"What did Dossin answer?"

"He laughed, and told Emile he was a sap."

"You work in the same street as the accused, don't you?"

"Yes."

"Before this date, the twenty-third of September, had you been seeing him almost daily?"

"Yes."

"And after it?"

"At first it was just the same as before...Then when he started going around with Nicole..."

Under his shapeless baggy trousers his knees were trembling.

"Go on...What happened then?"

"He didn't seem to have any further use for me."

"I see! He had reached his goal, had he?...Thank you... No further questions, Monsieur le Président."

Slowly Loursat rose to his feet.

Hostilities erupted over the very first question.

"Can the witness tell us how much pocket money his father gave him?"

Disconcerted, Luska turned toward the prosecutor, who made a movement as though to protest.

Without giving him time to do so, Loursat went on. "The prosecutor has questioned the witness, not merely on matters of fact but also on his opinions concerning my client's character. He surely cannot object if I in turn seek to reveal the character of the witness."

He had hardly finished when Luska flung back:

"He didn't need to give me any pocket money. I earned my own living."

"How much was Prisunic paying you?"

"Four hundred and fifty francs a month."

"Did you hand any of that over to your parents?"

"I gave my mother three hundred for my food and my laundry."

"How long had you been earning that much?"

"Two years."

"Did you put any money aside?"

Loursat seemed to fling his questions into the boy's face.

"Over two thousand francs."

"I see ... So the witness at the age of nineteen had saved over two thousand francs after working for two years."

And turning back to Luska, he snapped, "Did you have to buy your clothes with your hundred fifty francs?"

"Yes."

"Now, you put away approximately one hundred francs a month. That left fifty francs a month for everything including your clothes! ... Were you in the habit of cheating at cards too?"

Luska was losing his grip. He gazed as though hypnotized at this stumpy, bearded lump of a man who fired questions at him like cannonballs.

"No."

"Oh! Perhaps, like a previous witness, you helped yourself from the till in your father's shop?"

Even Emile was flabbergasted! Rogissart had an expression that showed that he thought this line of questioning was pointless, not to say scandalous, and he made a gesture to the president to intervene.

"I've never taken a sou from my parents."

The president was trying to get a word in, but Loursat ignored him.

"How often did you go out with Dossin and the others?"

"I couldn't say."

"Two or three times a week? I suppose, to say the least of it?"

Luska merely stared back at him, his eyes full of rancor.

"For something like eight months, wasn't it? That makes—"

The president rapped the table with his paper knife. Loursat broke off abruptly and turned toward him deferentially.

"I must remind you, Maître Loursat, that I am the only person entitled to interrogate the witness. Any questions you may wish to ask must be put to him through me."

"I beg your pardon, Monsieur le Président... Would you be so kind as to ask the witness who paid for him?"

Rather self-consciously, M. Niquet repeated, "Will you tell the jury who paid for you?"

"I don't know."

"Would you kindly ask him, Monsieur le Président, if the accused paid his way?"

Rogissart had wanted proper procedure to be observed. Now the president was forced to repeat everything in a comical fashion.

"Did the accused pay his way?"

"With the money he stole!"

Ten minutes earlier, the crowd had been listening apathetically to the witness's evidence. Now they were wide awake, following intently. They were unable to guess just what the fight was about, but the combatants were in the ring and that was enough. It wasn't Loursat's questions. They were harmless enough in themselves. It was the willpower behind them that electrified the onlookers.

Emile had been looking puzzled by his counsel's vehemence. Now a keen look crept into his eye. Was he beginning to understand?

Luska's eye had changed in expression too. The rancor was giving place to a hunted look. He felt himself to be all alone in the midst of a hostile world.

"I would like to know, Monsieur le Président, whether, up

to the events of which we are dealing, the witness had any relations with women."

The question sounded all the more incongruous when it
came from the president's enormous mouth.

And the sulky answer:

"No."

"Was that due to timidity, to a lack of interest in the other
sex, or rather to a spirit of economy?"

Rogissart jumped up. "Monsieur le Président, I suggest that
these questions—"

"Very well, Monsieur l'Advocat Général, we'll leave them for
the present and get on to the next point...At the time of
Emile Manu's joining the little band, was the witness in love
with Nicole?"

A silence. Luska swallowed.

"A witness suggested yesterday that he was. As the case pro-
ceeds, the importance of this question will become increasingly
evident...What I am trying to show, Monsieur le Président, is
that the witness was at that time a repressed individual, shut in
upon himself, and nursing a secret passion...He had not, like
his friend Dossin, sought to initiate himself by visiting a professional."

A murmur of protest from one side of the court, a buzz of
excitement from the public benches. Once again the president
brought down his paper knife but this time Loursat ignored it.

"Answer me, Luska...? After Big Louie's death, did you
have relations with Adèle Pigasse?"

Luska stood very still. He had turned very pale and he stared
at Loursat with wide open, unblinking eyes.

"Adèle Pigasse, who frequented the Boxing Bar and walked
the streets of Les Halles, has often been arrested; I hope that
she will soon be present in court."

"Do you have any more questions?" asked the president.

"A few more, Your Honor. Would you ask the witness why,

in the space of a few days, he found it necessary to sleep with this woman several times?"

"You have heard the question?"

"I don't know what he's talking about."

Emile was neither sitting nor standing. His hands gripped the railing, and he leaned forward, one arm held by a guard.

"Would you ask the accused—"

As Rogissart began to protest, Loursat continued, "Pardon me! Would you be so good, Your Honor, to ask the witness to disclose what he told the woman on a particular night?"

Loursat couldn't drop his gaze for an instant; to let up would have given Luska a chance to recover. One moment the boy was rigid, hard, sullen; the next he groped about him for something to hold.

"I didn't hear the response, Your Honor."

"Speak louder, Luska."

"I never went with Adèle," muttered Luska. "It's all a pack of lies."

"Monsieur le Président," began Rogissart.

But Loursat cut him short.

"Monsieur le Président, I must ask permission to pursue my cross-examination in my own way... Will you please ask the witness whether he was not in my house on the night of October seventh and whether he was not the person whom the accused saw in the passage of the second floor disappearing through a doorway."

Emile was gripping the rail so tightly that his knuckles were white. There was a deathly hush in the court. Not a movement. Yet no one was so completely still as Luska. He seemed to be made of stone.

The president waited. Everyone waited. It was almost as though they respected his silence. Loursat stood, a hand poised in midair, gazing at his victim with all the power at his command.

At last a voice which seemed to come from far away answered, "I wasn't in the house."

The audience sighed audibly, but it wasn't a sigh of relief. Rather it was one of impatience, if not of exasperation. Everyone looked at Loursat.

"Can the witness swear that he was at home at the time? . . . Will he look the accused in the face as he answers?"

"Silence!" ordered the president, whose nerves were getting a bit frayed.

No one had uttered a word. Only, some of the people at the back had shuffled their feet.

"Since you are unable to look the accused in the face . . ."

Luska swung slowly around and raised his head. As for Emile, he could no longer contain himself. His features distorted, he shouted:

"You murderer! . . . Coward! . . . You . . ."

His lips trembled. It looked as if he'd break down altogether. And all he could find to say was that one word:

"Coward!"

It was almost as if you could see the shiver go down Luska's spine and hear his teeth chatter. He looked terribly solitary as he stood there with hundreds of eyes trained on him.

How long did it last? . . . A few seconds? . . . Perhaps not even one.

Then the end. Collapse. So sudden, so unexpected that afterward no one could remember having seen him fall. The next thing they knew was that Luska lay in a heap on the floor of the witness-box, his head buried in his arms, making strange and horrible sounds.

And right in the middle of the court, presiding over the scene, was that grotesque mouth with its eternal involuntary grin!

Loursat sat down in his seat slowly, fumbled beneath his robe for a handkerchief, then mopped his brow and wiped his eyes. He turned toward Nicole, who sat behind him white as a sheet. "Thank God for that," he muttered. "I couldn't have stood it much longer."

It was an ugly scene, and the president, after a hurried consultation with his two assistants, adjourned the court, and the next moment the red-and-black-robed figures were beating a hasty retreat. The jury retired reluctantly, looking over their shoulders at the prostrate witness, over whom a couple of lawyers were bending.

Emile was led away, he too looking back, bewildered, anxious, unable to grasp the situation.

Loursat sat motionless in his seat, limp and sulky, nauseated by all the hatred he had brought to the surface by wading through these muddy waters, a hatred that did not belong to men but to boys. Petty humiliations...Petty envies...The want of a few francs...A pair of worn-out shoes.

"Really! To think they'll have to begin all over again!"

Loursat raised his big eyes toward the colleague who had questioned him. Did this concern him? There was a commotion in the corridor. Ducup bustled around, worried.

Not knowing how long the adjournment might last, the crowd sat tight, afraid of missing something.

"You ought to go out for a moment and get a breath of fresh air, Father."

Not, perhaps, the wisest thing to suggest! Never mind. It suited him all right. He was thirsty, terribly thirsty. Not caring who might see him, he went just as he was, in his robe, to the little bar with the good Beaujolais.

"Is it true what they're saying—that Luska has confessed?" asked the proprietor filling his glass.

Yes, yes. Of course it was. From now on, it would all be plain sailing. Luska would tell everything, more than they wanted to hear.

Had anyone understood that when Luska had sunk to the

floor it had been from lassitude? All he wanted was peace, and if he wept it had been with tears of relief.

At last he could escape from that unbearable solitude, from being alone with himself and with all those dirty little truths he alone knew. They would become different now, a real drama of life, or at any rate what people imagine drama to be.

No more haunting oppression, no more humiliation, above all no more fear!

Did he know himself why he had killed Big Louie? Perhaps not. That didn't really matter. Things would be explained otherwise, translated into decorous language.

His counsel would speak of jealousy, of unrequited love, of the hated rival who had stolen the object of his adoration.

Indeed he would do it so well that it would end by being true! . . . Almost beautiful!

Whereas, up to date, as he chewed the cud of his misery, it had just been the sordid envy of a poor and ill-favored Luska. Not an envy of the rich, of the people like Edmond Dossin to whom he could submit with willing servility, but of another like himself, one whom he had himself introduced to this select band, but who had walked right over him without even noticing it. Emile was a climber, while he, Luska, had been merely a rung.

"I think I'll have another," sighed the lawyer.

What time was it? He hadn't the faintest idea. Looking out into the street, he saw a funeral passing. Behind the hearse and on either side were the undertakers in their frock coats and cocked hats, and following them a straggling column of people in black. Watching them from the pavement were people from the Palais, lawyers in their robes, they too looking grave and ceremonious. And the two camps eyed each other with just a touch of antagonism, like the votaries of rival religious sects.

With drops of wine in his moustache, Loursat ordered a third glass. Someone touched his arm:

"The president's asking for you, Father."

She saw him hesitate and a beseeching look came into her eyes.

"One moment."

He gulped down his third glass and groped for his money.

"Don't bother, Monsieur Loursat. You can pay me another time... We haven't seen the last of you, I hope."

12

POOR PHINE! She was animated by such goodwill that her ugly face had become almost engaging.

"You really ought to join the party, Monsieur... And in any case you must have something to eat."

She couldn't even bring herself to look disapprovingly at the two bottles of burgundy or the innumerable cigarette butts scattered all over the study, reminiscent of the bad old days.

Loursat looked back at her with his big droll eyes.

"Yes... No... Tell them I'm tired, Phine."

"Monsieur Emile is so anxious to thank you..."

"Yes... Of course..."

"Then I'll tell them you're coming, shall I?"

"No... Tell them... tell them I'll be seeing them one of these days."

It was only what Nicole had expected, and she understood at once when she saw the disappointed expression on Phine's face. She forced herself to smile as she turned to Mme Manu to say, "I must ask you to excuse him. He's rather overdone. He's been working so hard these last weeks... Besides, you know, he's not quite like other people..."

Emile couldn't let that pass without saying, "He saved my life." And then, on a more homely note, "He's a great man."

Mme Manu was concerned, more than anything else, with her deportment. She sat at the dinner table a little too stiffly, a little too much on her best behavior.

"It's kind of you to have asked us here this evening. Of course I'm the happiest woman in the world, and yet—well, I can't help feeling that if Emile and I had been alone in our little house it would somehow have been rather sad."

She wanted to cry.

"If you only knew what I've suffered... When I think that my son..."

"But it's all over now, Mother."

He was still in his blue suit and dotted tie. Phine hovered around the table and saw to it that his plate was heaped high.

"After all you've been through in prison!" she seemed to be saying.

Now and again Nicole appeared to be listening for something and a faraway look came into her eyes. Emile noticed it and was almost jealous. Her mind, he felt sure, was constantly reverting to the person who was not there.

"What's the matter, Nicole?"

"Nothing."

It was difficult in a moment to pick up all the threads that had been interrupted.

"Have you told him I'm going to Paris?"

"Yes."

"What does he think about it?"

"That it's the best thing you could do."

"Does he agree to our getting married as soon as I've got a job?"

Why did he talk so much? Why was he in such a hurry to get everything said? She listened but there was nothing for her to hear except the wind in the chimney and the occasional scrape of knives and forks. Not Mme Manu's, of course. She didn't make a sound with hers. She held them lightly, as she ate daintily, hardly daring to bite.

"I can't think how he managed to find it all out... Still less how he got Luska to admit it..."

The veal was overcooked. Phine apologized for it, though she was hardly to blame, as she had had to see to everything. Yet another maid had been bundled out of the house that day, for speaking disrespectfully of Mademoiselle.

"Excuse me a moment, will you?"

Nicole almost slunk out of the room. In the dark passage she stopped suddenly on hearing the study door shut and then her father's footsteps. She slipped out of the way, concealing herself in a doorway, so that he trudged past her without suspecting her presence.

Or did he suspect it? If not, why was there that momentary hesitation in his walk? He breathed heavily. He had always breathed like that, doubtless because of all the wine.

He went downstairs, put on his hat and coat, unbolted the front door, and went out.

Nicole remained where she was for a moment. Then summoning a smile to her face—for she was happy, wasn't she?—she rejoined her guests.

"We're ready for the cheese, Phine."

Loursat walked along a sidewalk hardly wider than himself. He had no idea where he was going. It had taken hold of him all of a sudden as he was in the act of putting some more coal onto the fire. He had paused with the shovel in midair. He had looked around him and had suddenly felt himself a stranger to the background against which he had lived so long. Those books—hundreds of books, thousands of them, the heavy, thick atmosphere, the peace, the silence in which you could hear your own pulse beating.

He shuffled as he walked. He thought of Rogissart and his wife, and he couldn't help chuckling. They'd have to begin all over again! Ducup too. As for his sister Marthe, she must be in a flat spin at the idea of her precious Edmond having to go into the witness-box once again. She would certainly send for Dr. Matray.

He crossed the rue d'Allier and passed a brasserie in which they were playing billiards. He couldn't see the players, though he could hear the clack of the balls.

It was at a billiard table that Luska had met Edmond... And there was the shop, Luska's shop, in one wing of an old house. It had those old-fashioned wooden shutters that had to be put up every night. The shop light was not on, but a faint glow shone through the chinks in the shutters and under the door, coming no doubt from the single room behind, which served as kitchen, living room, and bedroom.

From a house opposite a young man emerged, happy to be off to the cinema.

Loursat couldn't very well look through the keyhole! Nor could he knock on the door and say to the man with the Bulgarian moustache:

"If you'd allow me, I'd be only too happy to undertake..."

No! Enough of that! Who could possibly understand such a thing? They'd merely take him for a madman. You don't offer to defend the very man you have just ruined. A man? No. A human being? Hardly. Rather a pawn in a game played by others.

He brushed past a policeman, who shrugged his shoulders on seeing him go into the Boxing Bar. What did he suppose the lawyer to be seeking?

"I thought you'd be coming along sometime," said Joe, "but I didn't expect to see you today... About that letter... I must explain... It seems that Gène did a job in Angoulème a couple of months ago, and he felt sure if Adèle was questioned she'd let something out... But I wish I'd been there when you got going. They say you were a holy terror!... What'll you have?... Yes, this is on me... And when Monsieur Emile comes to see me it'll be a bottle of champagne... He's got guts, that kid."

Loursat had lived alone too long! It takes time to get used to the human race. He was ill at ease. To cover up his awkwardness, he drank.

It occurred to him that he might feel more at home elsewhere, at the Auberge aux Noyés, for instance.

He went there. He returned there again on other nights until all the night taxi drivers got to know him.

He was no better off there, however.

Sometimes he would merely wander about the streets and once, when he saw all the lights on in the Dossins' house, he said to himself, "Suppose I rang and announced that I'd come to cut in for a rubber of bridge!"

He was really happiest drinking a glass of cheap spirits with La Morue, the old woman who lived at the bottom of the little alley off the rue de Poitiers, the one who let rooms to La Gourde and Adèle. For Adèle returned not long after, Gène having thought it more prudent to put himself on the other side of a border.

There in the squalid old building few words were spoken. When they were, they meant something, for their speakers were people who knew just about all there was to know. For the most part, however, you merely drained your glass and stared in front of you.

Adèle, since her reappearance, had taken to playing solitaire. She only heard once from Gène when she got a postcard from Brussels. With the dispersal of the Boxing Bar Gang, Joe's business suffered considerably, and he was talking of packing up and buying himself a stand in a traveling fair.

The most annoying thing was that Phine was insisting on going to join Mademoiselle when the latter set up house in Paris. That meant Loursat's having to cope with creatures like Angèle or someone suitable to a parish priest.

The streets around the marketplace seemed darker and narrower than ever, and, going along them at night, you got the impression you were tunneling right under the lives of ordinary people.

A new examining magistrate—for Ducup had been promoted to a better post—was apt to say, "Loursat? He certainly knows the town better than anyone else and what goes on beneath the surface." And then, if you looked at him inquiringly, he would add, "A pity that a man of such brilliant gifts..."

As his voice trailed off, you might just manage to catch the word, "...drink..."

Luska got ten years. His mother died. His father still sold marbles in the little shop that was smellier than ever.

A shiny picture postcard in harsh colors of Vesuvius belching flame and smoke bore on the other side:

Love from Naples
—Nicole and Emile

Edmond Dossin was in a luxurious sanatorium, his father in some smart nightclub with the girls, Destrivaux had shown such a grasp of regimental finance that he had been promoted to sergeant...

Ducup at Versailles, Rogissart at Lourdes for three days as a voluntary stretcher-bearer, young Daillat married to the daughter of a man who sold phosphates.

Adèle and La Gourde on their strip of sidewalk.

And Loursat, still dignified if somewhat the worse for wear, sitting all alone in a bar, in front of a glass of red wine.

TITLES IN SERIES